~ **A NEW BEGINNING SERIES** ~

MIDLIFE
CRYPTIC

MIA CONNOR

OTHER TITLES IN THE SAME SERIES

Midlife Dramatic

Midlife Ecstatic

Midlife Hypnotic

Midlife Cathartic

Midlife Magnetic

For information: www.miaconnorbooks.com

ISBN 978-1-914370-56-4

First Edition: August 2021

10 9 8 7 6 5 4 3 2 1

MIDLIFE CRYPTIC

1

IF I HADN'T BEEN SO BLINDED by my indignation back then, perhaps I would have seen the signs. Written in the stars. Aligned by the universe. Conspired by Fate. God knows what. But I just didn't see it then, that my past was calling out to me and my inner nature was struggling to surge to the surface after twenty long years.

Bonnie looked at me from across the table and raised the champagne flute in a toast. The effervescent liquid sputtered and hissed and looked inviting. Bonnie's warm smile seemed to be telling me that everything would be okay. But everything was NOT okay.

"Happy birthday, Im," Bonnie said, smiling at me expectantly. I managed to eke out a smile, knowing how hard my friend was trying to cheer me up, and raised my glass as well.

"Happy forty-second fucking birthday," I said in response, gulping down the champagne a bit too eagerly.

"Come on, Im. That's not the spirit," Bonnie chided. "I know you're going through a hard time, but we're going to pull through this. You have your job, you have your friends, you have two wonderful children. Think of it as a new beginning."

"Bonnie, it's just that I can't wrap my brain around what he's doing. I mean, a drinking problem? He has the audacity to imply that I have a drinking issue? I mean, these are legal papers! I could lose my kids!"

"Im, I hate to point it out to you but your kids are full blown adults. You're not going to lose them," Bonnie said with a slight grin.

But I wouldn't listen. The tirade continued. "He's grasping at straws. He's coming up with anything and everything to tear my children away from me and to take away as much money as possible. I've invested twenty years in this marriage, I deserve my fair due. Besides, I'm forty-two; I can't start over again."

"That bastard," Bonnie chimed in, chugging back the champagne in the flute and wiping her mouth carelessly with the back of her hands. "He has no class. As the mother of his children, no matter what, he shouldn't put these kinds of things on public record."

"But Bonnie, that's not even the point. It's not true!" I reiterated a bit too loudly. The people at the table next to me looked at me. Bonnie stared at me intently from behind a tangle of red curls that framed her face. A face that was shrouded in concern. Her eyes followed me slowly and carefully as I poured myself another glass of champagne. And drank it down like water.

"Go slow there, tiger," Bonnie warned, only half in jest.

I looked at her with a scathing gaze. "Go ahead, say it, Bonnie. Are you going to tell me I have a drinking problem too?"

"No, that's not what I was going to say."

"Then, what is it? Yes, I like to let loose once in a while, but that hardly means I go overboard. I mean, so does half of this city have a drink at the end of the day, it's not a big deal."

"Imogen, you're having this conversation with yourself. I never said any such thing. And it's your birthday. You're allowed to relax. And you've had some horrible news from that awful man."

And then, Bonnie's expression darkened, "Yes, I saw you fight a couple of times, but I knew better than to interfere in a married couple's life. Besides, you seemed so happy most of the time."

"Bonnie, you answer me first: What didn't you like about Devlin?" I pressed the matter, lubricated by the alcohol. I was curious, and I wanted to piece together the puzzle that was the broken bits of my marriage. How had things gone so very wrong over the last two decades? It hadn't all been so bad. But I wanted an outside perspective.

"Okay, well, I thought he was a bit arrogant. But only a little," Bonnie added quickly. "I also assumed that this was part of the, you know, business he was in. High finance. Real estate. That sort of wheeling and dealing. Handling all that money, no doubt, it must be heady stuff. But I'd always thought he treated you well, and you always seemed cheerful and smiling, and the children seemed so happy, so I didn't say anything."

I looked away, out the window, toward the Manhattan skyline. I couldn't experience the comfort it normally brought me. The glass and steel of the high rises and the people bustling about had always had a strange way of making me feel centered. Like I was in the middle of the universe. But not that night.

"It's hard to describe, Bonnie. When I'd met Devlin, I fell head over heels in love. He was the most handsome man I'd ever seen. He took my breath away. And he showered me with attention and love. You've got to understand, I'd just come from a small village in Scotland. And from an unhappy life. I was vulnerable, and I landed straight in the arms of this incredibly handsome, successful young man. He seemed to think the world of me. Those first few years were bliss. Everything felt preordained. The children came quickly, one after the other. I didn't have to worry about money, with my husband making his mark in the financial world."

I turned around and looked into Bonnie's eyes. "You know, I wasn't always this unambitious. I'd wanted to be a doctor back in Scotland. A surgeon. I almost became one, too. I got into medical school."

"Why didn't you go?" asked Bonnie, genuinely curious. I could immediately feel that part of me shutting down, the part that contained the secrets, the vast miasma of lies and concocted backstories and necessary illusions I needed in order to birth and sustain this new world I'd made for myself. There was no room for the truth of the past to surface. This shutting down, this lockdown mechanism was something I had become very familiar with over the last twenty years. So, I changed the subject. "Oh, I wanted to get out of that small world; I came from a small village as you know. And I wanted to see the world."

It was all lies. I knew I would have never left Perthshire if what had happened with my father and Michael hadn't happened. But when you tell yourself something is true, often enough, it starts sounding like the truth. It became my truth.

"Hmm," said Bonnie, not looking quite convinced, but knowing better than to press the subject. "Look, we've been friends for ten years now. I thank the gods that we met each other on that fateful day in the yoga studio. You remember that day?" Bonnie asked mischievously.

"Oh, how could I forget?" I said, looking at Bonnie." The yoga instructor was practically molesting you in the middle of the studio."

"He was not! He was teaching me the finer points of those complicated poses!" Bonnie protested vociferously.

"Oh, get off of it, Bonnie. He was gorgeous and you wanted him to put his hands all over you."

"Well, you didn't think anything about telling me that's exactly what you believed at the end of the session."

"Well, if I hadn't, we wouldn't have become friends, Bonnie," I said, staring affectionately at her. I loved Bonnie. It had been a friendship that had happened seamlessly and naturally, and it had stayed that way since that yoga studio day. And yet I'd kept a part of me away from her. A fundamental part. The Faerie part. She didn't know much at all about my childhood, except that I'd grown up in Scotland in a small village. Now, she knew I wanted to study medicine. It was indeed time to infuse the evening with new subject matter.

"Ladies, would you like to move on to some wine? We have an excellent list." The waiter had come up to us and had offered some tantalizing options.

"No, I think I'm good," said Bonnie.

"Actually, I think I'll have a glass of red wine, if you serve by the glass," I interrupted, trying not to make eye contact with Bonnie. "Something light and Italian."

"We have a wonderful Valpolicella from 2010," offered the waiter.

I knew it was going to be expensive, but it was my birthday. And I didn't know how much longer I had access to my wonderful husband's credit cards.

"What the hell? Get me a glass of that," I said, turning back to face Bonnie squarely, expecting some type of criticism. *You're drinking too much.* Or *You don't want to appear like you have a problem, especially when this divorce is up in the air.*

But Bonnie didn't say anything. She just stared at me lovingly, and said, "You're going to be fine. And the forties are when the real fun begins."

Bonnie had two kids of her own. Two teenage girls. "The kids are finally all grown up, and we can have some time to ourselves. And you've got your writing with the newspaper. I know it's more of a freelance position, but you can ask them to make it more permanent if you want."

I stared again, out the window. "Yeah, that's probably what I'm going to have to do. Bye-bye, fancy Upper East Side apartment," I said, waving out at the skyline.

"Is he really going to take the apartment away from you?" Bonnie asked, incredulous.

I looked at her. "Yes."

"The bastard. Why did it get so rancorous between you two? And when? Last month, you seemed okay at the opera."

"You know, Bonnie, I really don't understand it beyond a point myself. You know Devlin's always been reserved. But he'd always been affectionate toward me, and that's all I'd cared about. It stayed that way for many years. Then, at some point, a few years back, he started withdrawing from me. I tried to get him to talk about it, but it would only make him defensive and angry. And then, two summers ago, he started being abrasive with me. Nothing physical, but he would snap at me all the time. It was almost a kind of emotional abuse. And, no sir, I'm not the kind to take that kind of behavior. So, it led to fights and arguments. Finally, we were sleeping in separate rooms. I felt so bad that the kids, Lexie and Justin had to be there for the unpleasantness in the end, before they headed off to college. I really regret that. But this fall, with Alexis off to college as well, I guess the charade was up for him. I told him I couldn't go on like this, that we needed to get into couples counselling to fix this marriage and get to the root of the problems that were making him so aggressive toward me. And it was at that point ... " I paused and looked at Bonnie and said, "he said the most hurtful thing he'd ever said to me in twenty years of being together."

"What did he say?" Bonnie asked, gently.

"He told me he'd lost respect for me. That I'd given up on my dreams. And that he couldn't be saddled with someone who didn't want more from life."

Bonnie stared at me for a long moment, her eyes welling up with tears. And then she said, "Well, thank God you're rid of him. And what an absolute jerk to say something like that. You came from a foreign land, started life from scratch, raised two beautiful children, wrote these wonderful articles for the *Manhattan Times*. You've done so much, and yet, he says something so cruel to you. Pins the blame on you. Now, I'm not saying marriage, especially long ones, don't have issues, from time to time. But that he would clearly shift the blame onto you, speaks to his character. I'm glad you're rid of him, Im. Good fucking riddance."

"Yeah," I said, fidgeting with the rim of my wine glass. The sadness that had welled up within me was surging to the surface, and I wanted to move on.

"Let's not talk about this anymore, Bonnie. It's my birthday," I said, as if it were a blanket excuse to brush the rules that governed day-to-day life under the carpet. "Hey, did you see the papers? About that horrible murder in Central Park?"

Bony had stared at me blankly for a moment, and then said, "Oh, God, yes. It's all over the news. It seems like something out of a science fiction movie, doesn't it? That poor woman's body was literally ripped apart. Like an animal had torn into it."

"It's horrific," I said. "Who would do such a thing?"

"Who or what?" Bonnie said.

"Oh, come on, Bonnie, are you telling me that they're wild animals running around in the middle of Manhattan?"

Bonnie got animated. "No, I'm just saying, whoever would do that possessed the strength to physically render another human being asunder.

"There are a lot of freaks out there," I said. And then, I looked out the window again for the last time. "And it seems I've married one of them."

Bonnie and I burst out laughing. She raised her champagne flute and said, "Cheers to that!"

I raised my glass, drank a deep swig, and felt better inside.

2

THE MONOLITHS OF GLASS and steel seemed to rise up into the darkened heavens as I made my way unsteadily back to my apartment. Fifth Avenue glowed with the muted light of shop windows and the street lights and the offices winding down for the night. Well, the streets were still bustling.

The wine coursed through my veins, and I remembered feeling a warm glow inside. The kind of feeling that comes from spending an evening with a close friend. Even in those dark times, Bonnie had a way of making me see the bright side of things. Or at least putting them in perspective.

Yes, I was 42. The money in my bank accounts, which I shared with my husband, seemed to be rapidly dwindling. My children were away at college. And the income that I received from my intermittent work with *Manhattan Times* didn't provide me with enough to sustain the lifestyle that I'd become used to. Heck, it didn't provide enough money to sustain a decent living anywhere on this island! The divorce papers that had been served to me that morning had made things clear. If I wanted a fair share of the pie, so to speak, I was going to have to fight for it. And this meant hiring a lawyer. Lawyers were expensive. My head was spinning. And it all seemed too much to process.

I couldn't believe that I was in this position. There was a time when I loved my husband with all my heart and soul. But now he'd turned into a distant, almost mythical figure. A sinister enemy, covered with thorns, and threatening to hurt me at every turn. It suddenly dawned on me. *Devlin resented me.* But why? But what had I done to him? Yes, sometimes I would pull him up when I thought he was being arrogant. And sometimes I would tell him not to look down his nose at those people who were born into privilege. Devlin had come up the hard way, making his way first in Wall Street and then in the real estate business.

But every life was unique and different, I told him. Just because someone was born rich, it didn't mean that they were born without values or morals. Or that they even felt entitled to their lifestyle. But Devlin was a man of strong views. And now I could see how strongly he disliked me. But I didn't come from wealth. Maybe he thought I was taking the easy way out too. By allowing him to be the breadwinner. But I had raised his children. Our children. I thought that that was what he'd wanted. I'd had plans of becoming a world-renowned surgeon. Of healing people. I'd had plans that were never to bring me to these fatal shores. But that was a long time ago.

As I made my way past Sixty-Seventh Street, I admitted to myself that I'd perhaps drank a bit too much. And the distance to my home, a couple of blocks away, seemed interminably long. I thought of the comfort of my bed and of allowing all of this to wash away into oblivion. Into sleep. However, when I reached the entrance to my apartment building, the doorman informed me that there was a visitor. It was ten past ten. Who could it have been? I entered the building to find a very tall, strikingly handsome man with red hair and green eyes staring at me intently. He jumped to his feet upon seeing me. And when the doorman informed him of who I was, he came forward to introduce himself.

"Hello. Imogen McLelland? I'm Eoin McLaren. You don't know me, but I was sent to speak to you by someone from Killin."

He waited with paused breath, observing my reaction. I'd been completely taken aback. I hadn't heard someone mention the name of my hometown in decades. Someone with a local Scottish accent. I'd never brought it up with my children, and my husband knew better than to ask me about it. Yet, here was a man claiming to be from my hometown in faraway Scotland and who wanted to talk to me. It felt surreal.

"Is there somewhere private that we can go so we can discuss an urgent matter?" Eoin said with a familiar melody that brought a surge of homesickness to well up from within unexpectedly. In

Manhattan, we're not used to letting strangers into our apartments, but something told me it would be okay to do it this one time. Besides, the doorman had seen him. I nodded and pressed the elevator button and let Eoin in and followed silently behind. The smell of his cologne lingered in the air in the elevator, and I took the time to look him squarely in the eyes.

"What is this about?" I couldn't wait to ask and blurted out the question. My curiosity had been piqued.

"I'm afraid this concerns your mother. Mary." The moment he said those words, I felt as if the floor beneath me had opened up and I was in free fall. The tiny cubicle of an area we were trapped in started spinning.

"Is she all right?" I asked immediately. "Is mum all right?" I repeated.

Eoin nodded his head. I was flooded with relief.

"She's okay, but only just."

The elevator doors opened and I quickly let him into my apartment. I turned on the lights and then spun around to confront him.

"What do you mean 'She's only just barely okay?' If something has happened to mum ... "

Eoin stared at me blankly for a long moment and then said, "Well, it has been twenty years, Imogen."

He looked weary and sat down on the sofa nearest to him without asking.

"Your mother is suffering from cancer. Breast cancer. She's had surgery. And chemotherapy. But she's in remission." The words echoed in my head. There was the beginning of a searing pain from deep within my body, and I quickly tried to quell it. I felt nauseous.

"Why didn't anyone inform me?"

"You left without even saying goodbye to her. You haven't contacted her in decades."

"I know what I've done!" I shouted, rubbing my hands together, which suddenly felt very cold.

"She didn't want you to know you. Besides, the community was there for. Her friends really chipped in." I felt sick to my stomach.

"What do you mean, the community? What about my father? Mark?"

"Mark and Mary separated a few years ago, Imogen. They're no longer together. He moved out."

All of this was too much to process.

"Did something happen?" I asked Eoin and, at this, he turned away and looked out the window. He didn't have to say anything to me. I understood what this meant. For years, I had seen my mother suffer silently, burying the body blows from her inebriated husband. And while it was not openly discussed, in that instant, it became clear to me that it was an open secret in the village of Killin. Mary was a battered wife. My heart felt like it was breaking into a million little pieces.

"She is at home now," Eoin offered, changing the subject. "She has a home healthcare provider who takes care of her needs. But that's the reason why I'm here. Imogen, your mother wants you to come and see her before anything happens. She thought about writing a letter to you, or an email. But she was fearful that you wouldn't respond. She sent me personally, to convince you to come back."

"And how are you connected to my mother?" I asked Eoin, suspiciously, but mostly with a broken heart.

"I'm not," he replied, rather honestly. "I run the local bookstore. The Literatus. Your mother used to come in to buy a lot of books. We became friends. When she heard I was coming into New York City on work, she asked me if I would do this for her." Eoin extracted a letter from his coat pocket. "It's from your mum. She wanted me to hand-deliver it to you. I, of course, said yes."

I opened the letter and, on seeing the familiar handwriting, burst into tears. I closed it again, hastily. "I just can't read it now," I said, looking tormented.

"I understand," he said.

"Thank you," I offered meekly. "For conveying this message."

I sat down wearily on the sofa opposite to where Eoin was sitting. It didn't occur to me to even offer him a cup of tea or water.

I did want to see my mum. I ached for her. I loved my mother. But I was scared to visit my past.

Dead scared.

In it, lay trauma that'd been buried so deep, I was viscerally afraid of its exhumation. Giving up my old life and coming here to America and starting again from scratch was the hardest thing I'd ever had to do. I'd hidden my Faerie heritage from the people closest to me: my family. I did plan on telling my children soon. But other than that, I'd become completely American. I could hardly recall the life before. That way of being.

But Eoin looked unimpressed with my tears. "I'm sorry you're struggling with this, Imogen. But she is your mother. And besides, I've been told none of us can run away forever from the things that haunt us. They will inevitably catch up with us, as this has to you."

I stared at the handsome man showering me with these harsh words even as I was crying a pool of tears, as he simply fidgeted with his fingers and looked out the window. And suddenly, I had another overwhelming rush of homesickness. Hearing his accent. Listening to him talk of life back in my small Scottish village. It was all too much.

"How much time does my mother have?" I asked Eoin, knowing it was a cruel but natural question.

"It's not like that. Like I said, she's in remission."

"Oh," I said. "Yes, she's doing okay. But she is not cured of cancer, nor will she ever be. The clock is ticking. She would like to spend some time with her daughter. That is all."

With those words, Eoin got up and started making his way toward the door. "My job was to convey this message to you. How you choose to act upon it is up to you."

Before he left, he turned around and asked, "How old are your children?"

"Justin is nearly twenty and Alexis is eighteen. They're both at university now."

"And your husband? Where is he? At work?"

"Oh, Devlin." I decided against sharing the details of my personal life.

"He's away on work," I lied.

"And they don't know anything about your past?"

"Very little."

"I meant your Faerie past."

With that, it became clear to me in an instant that I was in the presence of a faerie. A kindred spirit. It changed everything. I just stared at him.

"Yes, I'm of the fellowship," he offered, looking nonplussed.

I took a deep breath.

"No, nothing of the Faerie past."

It suddenly occurred to me that I hadn't offered this gentleman, who'd come all this way to convey a message, and with nothing to gain in return, even a measly glass of water or a cup of tea.

"Can I offer you something to eat or drink?"

"Actually, I'm starving, but not to worry. I think I'll go around to the bistro I saw around the corner. I also want to meet an old friend. I thought I would give him a call and ask him to join me. I believe he lives around the corner."

Before leaving the door, Eoin turned around and stared at me intently. "Would you like to join us?"

I'd already had dinner, but something about this tall, brooding man made me want to spend more time with him. Perhaps it was because he made me feel close to my home. My original home.

"I could grab a drink, I guess, as I've already had dinner."

"I wouldn't want to put you out."

"No, not at all. I'll grab my coat and purse," I said.

We walked out the door even as I was a cauldron of churning emotions, inside. There was, again, that whiff of the cologne. Something about it was so familiar. It reminded me of the Scottish hillside and the birds singing as twilight descended on the village of Killin. And of laying carefree, as children, on the meadows. Of Michael. I looked at the beautiful stranger that had transported me back to my hometown in my mind's eye and wondered what sort of life he'd lived. Was he married? I needed to distract myself from the news I'd heard of my mother and, always the escapist, I was hoping my conversations with Eoin would lead to more insights into his mind and into life back in my beloved hometown. I'd hoped the night would be long and would unveil many more secrets from our shared Faerie past.

3

THE BISTRO WAS BUSY even at half past ten. However, we managed to find a quiet corner to sit down. Eoin sat across from me, nervously fidgeting with his cell phone. I stared at him intently. He was fine featured with slightly thinning red hair. And his green eyes sparkled in the dim, glowing light of the room. There were whispers of voices around us, but my attention had been focused entirely on this strange and magical entity that had appeared in my life from the past and had been the harbinger of heartbreaking news.

"Have you called your friend?" I asked Eoin.

"Yes. He said he'll be here in around fifteen minutes."

"Does he have a name?" I asked.

"Max. Max Murphy," Eoin replied, still fidgeting with his phone.

"Are you having trouble with your phone?" I asked.

"No."

He seemed uncomfortable around me. Or maybe he was just tired.

"Do you come to New York often for work?"

I tried to engage him in conversation, unsure if this was something he'd wanted to do. I'd clearly already created a bad first impression. *Spoilt, selfish, unfeeling daughter.*

"I'm here for a publisher's convention. But these things usually amount to people congregating at the bar and getting drunk. Actually, that's where most of the work gets done," Eoin said, managing a small smile.

"What sort of a bookstore do you own? Would I have seen it?" I asked gingerly.

"Imogen, it's been a long, long time since you've set foot in Killin. A lot has changed." Eoin immediately regretted what he'd said. "I'm sorry, I didn't mean to make you feel bad. I just meant that the times have changed. The village is bursting at its seams with population. Tourism is the main industry now. There are many more shops on the high street, a lot more bars and pubs and discotheques."

"Discotheques?" I asked, surprised. "There weren't any back when I was growing up. But I still had a burning question. "Mark. My dad, where is he?"

"Oh, he moved to a neighbouring village. He's still the president of the Building Council of Perthshire. But Mary and him—

they went their separate ways a few years back. She'd had enough of him." Eoin noticed me staring at him intently.

"He has a new family now, Imogen," he said bluntly. Strangely, I didn't feel shocked at that news. The only thing that went through my veins was sorrow that my mother had been left to fend for herself after an unhappy and violent marriage. And then dealing with cancer. And her only daughter had fled her side, never bothering to check in. If I had allowed myself to let the guilt break through the barriers, it would have overwhelmed me. I'd learned over the years to keep it at bay, through any means. I'd developed a coping mechanism, distancing myself from my past to the extent that it seemed like it had happened to another person.

And yet here I was, sitting with a man from my own village. And one who knew of my Faerie heritage.

"Are you a faerie?" I asked Eoin.

He rolled his eyes. "I thought that was a given by now. Of course, I am Imogen. You know, we are sworn to a secret pact not to reveal our identities to those outside the fellowship. What else could I be?" He seemed mildly irritated at my obtuseness.

"What sorts of books do you sell?" I changed the subject, feeling embarrassed.

"Oh, odds and ends, really. Mostly genre fiction: romance, mysteries, thrillers. I try to avoid fantasy fiction. Seems a bit too close to home," he said, chuckling.

"No Heathcliff on the moors?" I asked, smiling.

"Oh, the young ones will never go for that."

"Would you like to wait to order for your friend?" I asked.

"No, I'm quite hungry. I'm going to go ahead and order. What would you like to order?" he asked me, flipping through the menu.

I was tempted to order a glass of wine. Or maybe a pint of beer, but I decided against it. Given the heavy drinking earlier in the evening I decided to be responsible.

"I'm just going to get a cup of coffee."

I was eager for information about home. "How is the Faerie High Council doing these days?"

"Oh, up to the usual ways. Trying desperately to ensure the old ways survive, but the number of members are going down. People are marrying outside of the community. The High Council still meets once a year up in the Northern Highlands. I try to go to the meetings."

I was surprised to hear this. "You make the trek all the way to the Highlands each year? You must be a pretty important member of the council then?"

"Oh, I don't know that I'm important. I think I'm just useful to them. I have my little bookshop in the centre of town and nothing much escapes me. I've managed to integrate myself well into the regular way of life. And I have all the time in the world while waiting for customers to help out in little ways. That is one of the reasons I'm here, Imogen, to help out one of our own. I grew close to your mother when she was in the throes of cancer. She's a wonderful woman. She deserves to see her daughter. To see what you've become."

"What I have become," I repeated those words, cynicism lacing my breath.

"And what have you become? Your mother mentioned that you wanted to be a doctor very badly when you were young."

I smiled bitterly at him. "No, I'm not a physician. I never will be. When I left everything and came here to New York, I had to begin from scratch. There wasn't any money. I took jobs wherever I could find them. Dug into the arduous process of getting my citizenship. But then I met Devlin. My husband. And everything changed."

"Tell me about it," pressed Eoin.

I resigned myself to telling the story of my young romance, clouded now, with the bitterness of regret and rancor.

"I met him at a bus stop nearly two decades ago. I thought he was the most handsome man I'd ever seen, with his rakish grin and piercing blue eyes. I thought he'd walked out of a magazine catalogue," I said, giggling. "We fell instantly in love and had children very soon. He was a hardworking executive in the real estate business in his early thirties. Back then, I didn't know how ambitious he was. But in a few years, he really made his mark and started his own company with a few friends. Now, they develop some pretty important properties all across Manhattan."

"He sounds quite the catch," observed Eoin.

"Well, he's made a lot of money. And I had his kids. I don't mean to sound cynical; I love my children more than anything in the world. They are what keep me grounded. But now that they've left home, I guess you could say I'm looking for a new purpose."

Eoin kept staring at me. I didn't know what it was. Perhaps it was the expression on his face, or perhaps it was how sincere he looked. Or that we shared the secret bond with the Faerie fellowship. Or maybe, that we both came from the same actual village in Scotland. But I let my secrets spill out.

Looking down at the coffee on the table, I said, "The truth is, Eoin, I'm going through a bit of a rough patch. My husband has filed for divorce. Things haven't been working out for a while. And we're separated now. He's moved into a separate flat. I was served divorce papers this morning, actually! It's my forty-second birthday today. Happy birthday to me!" I said laconically. I picked up the cup of coffee, as if I were making a toast.

Eoin stayed silent for a long time and then said, "I'm sorry to hear this, Imogen. It's tough to make a new start, especially as we get older."

"Do you have a family of your own?" I asked him, curiosity getting the better of me.

"No, no, I've always preferred the single life. I'm most comfortable ensconced in my books. I never wanted the complication of family life. And all the responsibilities it brings."

"And yet, you're caring," I said. "You were willing to do this incredible favor for your friend. My mother."

"I *am* caring, Imogen. I just don't care enough to have children of my own."

I thought back to the last two decades of my life, and I couldn't imagine them without my children. In fact, maybe that had been the problem. Taking Justin and Alexis out of the equation, perhaps there wasn't much left in my marriage with my strikingly handsome husband. As I was pondering these thoughts, Max arrived. I was surprised to see that he was a policeman, still in uniform.

"Detective Max Murphy! It is a pleasure indeed, old chap," Eoin brightened up on seeing his friend. He got up and gave him a warm hug.

"Eoin, what's happening with your hair, mate? Thinning out quite badly, there!" Max joked with his friend and they both chuckled.

"Time hasn't been particularly kind to you either, Max. What's with the paunch?"

As the friends exchanged pleasantries and jokes, I couldn't help but wonder how a small bookstore owner from Killin had befriended a New York detective.

"Max, I'd like to introduce you to Imogen McLelland. Oh, I'm sorry, I don't know if it's still McLelland. She's a friend of mine from back in Killin. She's lived in New York City for several years now, decades in fact.

"Pleasure to meet you, Imogen. That's a beautiful name."

"Thank you," I accepted the compliment. Max was friendly and warm, and I immediately took a liking to him. He pulled up a chair and sat down at the small table we were placed at, and said to Eoin, "Do you know it's been nearly three years since we last met? Now, that's just inexcusable."

"Yes, I'm sorry, mate. But I hardly find a reason to leave my room, much less make a trip across the Atlantic to come to New York. You could've come and visited me."

"Well, you know how that went the last time," Max said, and after a pause, they both burst out laughing. There was a story there, and I was curious to find out what it was.

"You were in Scotland a while ago?" I asked Max.

"Yes, I was sent there to assist on a case. For Scotland Yard and we—Eoin and I—we ended up meeting in Sterling. We worked on the case together."

I was confused. "Wait. Eoin helped you with a police case?"

"It's a long story, Imogen," Eoin interrupted.

"But I'd be happy to share it over a pint of beer," said Max, mischievously.

I relented. We ordered a couple of rounds of beers, and Max ended up telling me the story of how he had crossed paths with Eoin in Scotland.

"So, you see, I was in a lot of trouble, and time was running out. I thought I was going to be murdered. Then, the next thing I knew, Eoin appeared out of nowhere and ushered me out of the room, straight out of danger. It was as if his presence silenced the room. It was like the room fell into a trance."

I'd heard of this before, that some faeries possessed the ability to put people into a trance of sorts. Some extremely special faeries. Max continued. "It was as if the room went deathly silent and everybody was in a stupor. But I'm referring to people actually becoming lethargic and sitting very still in their chairs, people who, up until a few moments ago, were extremely agitated and ready to break my neck. You rescued me and saved me that day, buddy. And when I asked him how he'd managed to do that, he told me he could either give me the honest answer, or not answer the question at all. But either way, I'd have to keep it a secret for the rest of my life. Or else, he'd have me killed, himself!" Max chortled and continued.

"Eoin told me about the Faerie fellowship, and given what I'd seen, I believed him. Everything seems mystical in Scotland anyway," Max said with a smile, gulping down a large swig of beer. He wiped his mouth with the back of his hand.

"Not like the nitty gritty, dirty realities of life in Manhattan. I've just come from a horrific crime scene. And I'm really grateful for this beer after what I've seen. Torn limbs and shattered skulls."

"Max, we're in the presence of a lady here," protested Eoin.

"Is she also…?" Max asked Eoin, leaving the question unfinished.

And before I could say anything, Eoin responded. "Yes, she is a faerie, Max."

I felt my cheeks flush with anger. Eoin hadn't even consulted me before revealing my identity.

"Oh, it's okay, Imogen. He won't tell anyone. He owes me big."

"But it wasn't your secret to share, Eoin," I said, bristling with tension.

I was rankled by the liberty the stranger had taken with my life, something that, to my ire, didn't seem to faze him at all, but at the same time it made me feel part of a secret coterie. A place where I could speak freely. And not pretend anymore.

"So, what are your special powers?" Max asked me.

After taking a very long moment to adjust to this new dynamic in conversation, I said, "I don't try to exercise that part of my brain at all if I can help it. It's been so long since I thought of myself as that...you know, a faerie. But I suppose I can see deeply into people. When I choose. And figure out their true nature. It's not a perfect power, clearly, given the impending demise of my marriage and my husband proving to be a complete stranger."

"Oh, I'm so sorry to hear this," Detective Max offered awkwardly.

"I'm not gifted like you, Eoin, and I can't put a room into a trance. You're really special, you know, if you can do that."

"The strength in our powers lies in our acceptance of our heritage, Imogen. The more you resist your true nature, the less potent your force becomes," Eoin said, staring at me intensely. It was almost as if he was taunting me, but at the same time, I liked the way his eyes felt on my body. It was comforting.

"Well, I haven't thought about that part of my life in a long time. I've been living the American dream, married to a rich husband. Two beautiful kids. More money than I knew what to do with. Well, up until this morning, anyway."

When the two gentlemen stared at me inquisitively, I continued. "I've been pressed with divorce papers, and my darling husband of twenty years seems to want most of everything, claiming he's earned it all. Paid for it. Then, there's some other unfair things he's accusing me of. I'd rather change the subject. Doesn't make for pleasant talk."

"I'm sorry to hear all of this," Max reiterated, chugging down the last of his beer. "He sounds like an asshole."

I should have been offended, but I chuckled.

"Actually, he was really good to me for the first part of our marriage. Nothing specifically happened, he just grew distant over the last few years. And when I tried to get him to open up about it, he would just grow hostile toward me. I couldn't take the temper. I've seen what terrible tempers do to marriages," I said, staring at Eoin. He understood.

"Was he ever violent? Let me know and I'll pay him a visit," Max offered.

"No, no, nothing like that. He was just rude and irascible and constantly provoking fights, but above all, he made me feel very small, like I hadn't contributed at all toward the success of my family."

There was a long pause where only the munching of the sandwich could be heard. I relented and ordered another beer, and I drank it down greedily as well, letting the alcohol do its work. This was one of those nights I wasn't going to keep track of how much I was drinking. For whatever reason, I wasn't getting drunk, so I didn't care. I guess I'd paced myself. But the melancholia inevitably set in. And I was eager not to give too much away.

"Tell me about these murders. I mean, if you can, that is."

"A woman's body was found in Central Park."

"Oh, my God, I said, suddenly waking up to visceral alertness. Bits of her body—she was torn asunder. Like an animal ripped her up."

"Wait, hold on. Is this the story that came in the papers? I know about this one. Are you saying...?" I left the sentence unfinished, unable to process what I was hearing.

"Yes, a second one. It's happened again. Just last night. Two women have been murdered so far, three days apart, in the depths of Central Park, and at night. In the most horrific manner. They were hunted down, bludgeoned to death and then their bodies and limbs were torn apart. Additionally, there were bite marks all over their bodies. There's no mistaking these were the crimes perpetrated by the same criminal, or criminals."

"It almost sounds like an animal had its way with them," I offered, disturbed.

"That is exactly what we were thinking. But there are no beasts in Central Park. Not the four-legged kind, anyway, that can bludgeon a human. But the bite marks make the matter confusing. Anyway, the bodies have been sent to the coroners for more examination. I really shouldn't be talking about the case. At all. It's against the law. Please keep this to yourself. Although it will be out in the news despite our best efforts. The city will go into a panic."

I listened intently. "Have you got any suspects?" I couldn't help but feel vulnerable, given that I walked by the fringes of the park every day to get to my apartment. The murders must have happened very, very close to where I lived.

"We rounded up a few people. But nobody seems to fit the profile. But we are testing DNA and blood samples. And fingerprints and dental impressions. It has to have been somebody in the city."

"Why do you say that?" I asked Max.

"I don't know, it's just a gut feeling. Like he's trying to send a message. The similarities between the murders. The location in an iconic park. He's somehow tied deeply, closely to the city. It's all quite horrific," Max said, finishing up the last crumbs of his sandwich.

"What do you do Imogen?" Max asked, suddenly. "I mean, do you work?"

"It's not a very polite question, Max," Eoin interrupted.

"Oh, I don't mind," I said. "I freelance for the *Manhattan Times*. I write for them quite regularly on current matters. Even on fashion and lifestyle."

"That's interesting," said Max, distractedly. Then he looked at me as if a light had gone off inside his brain. "You can see into people, right?"

"Well, that's putting it simply," I said.

"Yeah, okay. So, do you think, if we lined up a bunch of people, you'd be able to sense something sinister about any of them?"

I'd never thought about this before: using my powers for detective work.

"Well, Max, I don't know if I can switch it on and off like that. Besides, I'm really rusty. I hardly think of myself as a faerie anymore. And, as Eoin pointed out, the less you use your powers, the less potent they become."

"Yes, but do you think you could try? If I were to ask you to come in once in a while, when I talk to people or take a look at samples of things. Stuff connected to people involved with crime, do you think you might get a sense? As to whether they have been involved with the crime or not? This could be regular work and we could pay. Not much, but a small amount of money for it."

"Max, leave the woman alone. She's going through a challenging time in her life. With major upheavals."

"No, no, hold on. What kind of money are we talking about here?" I asked Max, interrupting Eoin. I knew I had a messy divorce coming up, and I could use whatever money I could lay my hands on to pay the lawyers. The truth was, I was frightened. And the prospect of making money seemed reassuring.

Eoin looked unimpressed.

"Well, a couple of hundred dollars a week. Does that sound good to you?"

It did. I took a long pause and then said, "Let me think about it. Can you give me a few days?"

"Sure, take the time you need," said Max. "Listen, I better be getting back to the station. It's abuzz with activity given what's happened. This latest discovery tonight in the woods. Imogen, here's my business card. You know how to find me when you're ready. Eoin, dear friend, it's been wonderful meeting you. How long are you in New York? Can we meet up again? Man to man."

"I'm afraid I leave tomorrow night, mate."

"Why such a brief visit?"

"As I told you, I'm not comfortable traveling. I like being home as much as I possibly can and stay away from it as little as I possibly can. But it's been wonderful seeing you. Please come and visit me in Scotland soon. Well, in the meantime, try not to get yourself into too much trouble, though."

With that, the men embraced each other deeply and bid their goodbyes. Max waved to me, kissed me lightly on the check, and then left the bistro.

Eoin and I sat down again. He looked serious, again. "Imogen, I hope you're not seriously considering this? If you work with the NYPD, at some point people will start questioning where you're getting all this insider information from. You stand at the risk of exposing your very nature. And that could make you very vulnerable, put you at risk. This isn't a safe city for you to be brandishing your supernatural powers. And besides, I didn't come here to get you a job. I came here to beseech you to go home and visit your ailing mother."

"I get the message, Eoin," I said testily. "But I'm close to losing everything that I've worked for my whole life. My world is collapsing, and if I need to make some income along the way so that I can stand up to the top lawyers my husband has hired so that not everything is taken away from me, can you blame me? And also so he doesn't turn my children against me. I will do what I have to do. I understand about my mother. But that's a private decision I'm going to have to make."

"What's there to decide, Imogen? Eoin asked impatiently. "She's your mother."

"I don't need you to tell me who she is to me," I said, snapping back. The truth of the matter was it was a well I just couldn't bring myself to dive into, for I knew what I'd done twenty years ago. I'd abandoned my mother. The person I loved the most in the world so I could give myself a brighter future. It was something that inspired such deep shame in me that I'd bottled it up. And the risk of opening that wound again meant facing up to the cowardly act, and it seemed too much for me to cope with. I didn't think my mind could handle it.

"I just needed some time to think about this, okay?" I said to Eoin. I was completely perplexed by his presence. He seemed like a sensitive man. And when he stared at me with the intensity he did, there was this illogical urge to run into his arms. He seemed like someone who could offer protection from everything that I was feeling. But that was what I had done once before. Twenty years ago. And look where it had brought me. No, I was going to stay strong. And I would deal with what I had to do with my mother, soon. First, I had to handle the family that I had made for myself here, in New York, and there were bills that needed to be paid to lawyers that would fight my case. I would have a deep think about it. I knew I had instantly fallen in Eoin's eyes. I could see it in his face. I couldn't blame him. He suddenly looked very distracted and said it was getting late.

"I need to get back to the hotel, Imogen. I have a long day tomorrow at the conference, then I fly out late tomorrow night. I've conveyed what I was meant to, it's up to you now, as a grown woman, to make the decisions you need to."

"I understand," I said. There was suddenly a stillness, a silence in the air, which had been filled with a lot of conversation, till up to a few minutes ago. I paid the bill, even though Eoin offered, and we bid each other goodbye.

At the entrance of the restaurant, I saw him turn left and walk away into the cold night, away from the bistro that skirted to the edges of the park, the park in which horrific crimes had been committed, just a few hours ago. I stared at Eoin's lanky figure until it disappeared into a sea of humanity heading home for the evening.

I turned around and faced the park, straight. And suddenly, I was overcome with a wave of something chilling. It iced me to the bone. There was a darkness in the air. I couldn't quite put my finger on it, but there were stirrings in me that were responding to something evil. Something sinister that lurked amidst the regular folk that peppered the streets. I pulled my winter coat close to my body, turned right, and briskly started walking home, grateful for the fact there were lights and people around me.

4

VISITS WITH MARSHA ALWAYS filled me with a sense of foreboding. My mother-in-law had the ability to press on my buttons in the most insidious of manners. And this would happen in the best of times. *This*, right now, was not the best of times. As I climbed up the walkway apartment stairs, I was filled with dreary dread and wondered what surprises awaited me in the form of the subtle barbs and quiet put-downs that were Marsha's specialty.

I rang the doorbell and stood outside, looking at my feet. I'd walked quite a distance in the melting snow, and the slush had left its imprint on my expensive boots. I wondered how many more times I would be able to afford buying those kinds of boots. My Neiman Marcus days were over. Marsha opened the door and to my surprise, seemed extremely happy to see me. She rushed to embrace me and ushered me into the apartment with the zeal of a VIP's visit.

"Darling child, you're shivering. You should get yourself a proper winter coat. Can I make you a cup of tea?" Marsha offered, solicitously. The apartment was warm and cozy, with a smattering of couches and the old grandfather clock on the side of the broken piano. It was the kind of apartment that reminded you that you were in a house that carried very old memories.

"No, Marsha, I'm good. Thank you," I said, and sat down, upon removing my coat and draping it over the side of the sofa. She sat near to me on the same sofa and turned around to face me.

"How are you, darling? It must be very difficult right now."

She was referring to the fact that her son had sent me divorce papers, the terms of which she would've been well aware of, knowing Marsha's close bond with Devlin, her only child. If one didn't know the intrepid old woman, you'd think that this was a kind thing to inquire, given that I was now the "enemy." The person being estranged from her son. But Marsha was not a simple woman. I knew her cheerfulness hid something deeper. There was always an ulterior motive to her behavior. She was a complex mother-in-law, and not one to be dealt with casually.

"Oh, I'm okay. Actually, come to think of it, that cup of tea sounds good. I'm shivering," I said.

"Coming right up." Marsha rushed into the kitchen. The apartment had an open plan, and I could see her putting the kettle on the stove. There was some time to kill, so she came back into the living room and said, "I should let you know I was just as shocked about this. As shocked as anyone. I thought the two of you were so happy. And the poor kids. Justin and Alexis, so young. So, so young. This is really going to take a toll on them. What happened between the two of you? Or is that too private a question to ask? Well, I am his mother, after all," she prattled on endlessly, glancing around the room, nervously.

She patted down the front of her dress. Marsha was a plump woman with curly, silver-grey hair. And, from what I knew of her, there was never a quiet moment in her head.

"I don't know how forthright I should be with you, Marsha," I said, "but the truth of the matter is, I was quite taken aback myself. I mean, we were having problems. We'd drifted apart, and there were fights over it. But I'd always thought we'd stay together till the end. I had the urge to tell her about how her son was squeezing me for every dollar in the divorce with a vicious ferocity that had stunned me. How he was clinically going about his divorce proceedings, trying to ensure I was left with only the minimum amount of savings to support myself. That he was even going after our marital home. But then I stopped myself from saying any of these things.

"Marriage can be tough," Marsha offered vaguely. "Peter and I went through a series of ups and downs as well, don't be fooled, but things were different those days. We stuck together no matter what. And Peter was a good-looking man. Trust me, he'd had quite a few female admirers that I had to fend off."

This disconcerted me. Why was she offering this peculiarly specific titbit of information? "Why would you mention this, Marsha?" I asked.

Suddenly, her face went ashen.

"Oh, nothing really. I was just commenting on the fact that marriages can be difficult and complex."

I knew Devlin could be difficult and demanding and arrogant. I knew he could be distant and sullen. But I'd always thought of him as faithful. But now Martha was introducing new thoughts into my head.

"Has he said something? Is Devlin seeing someone else?" I blurted out.

"Imogen, I don't think I'm the one you should be asking these questions."

"Wait, hold on. Are you saying he has a girlfriend?"

"I'm saying no such thing, Imogen. All I meant was, it takes two to make a marriage work."

"But I gave him everything Marsha," I said, hot tears of indignation welling up. "Twenty years of my life. I'd just arrived, fresh off the boat from Scotland. I opened my heart to him, I had his children. I gave up on having a more ambitious career for him."

"Nobody asked you to do any of that," Marcia snapped defensively. This was the true Marsha. I was stunned.

"And he gave you a very good life, didn't he? The best in shopping, restaurants and an Upper East Side apartment. A fancy education for your children. What more could you want?"

"I want answers!" I screamed. "Why did he just give up on the marriage without fighting for it? I know you know something, Marsha. And perhaps it's unfair to put the mother of a son in this position, but please don't pretend you're sympathetic toward me when you're clearly not!"

There was a long, stony silence. The grandfather clock in the corner of the room clicked away silently, counting the seconds.

"Look, Marsha, I know he's your son and you're going to defend him. And I'm not saying I'm perfect. Something has gone horribly wrong. I sense it in my bones. Nobody just gives up without an explanation. Nobody."

And then, I saw it. In the corner of my vision, placed on a credenza. There was a framed photograph of Devlin and a beautiful blond woman, holding each other tightly. They seem to be out at sea.

"Who's that?" I asked, walking toward the photo frame. Martha looked flabbergasted.

"Oh, Imogen. It's not what you think. That's just, that's just … "

I picked up the photo and looked at it closely. It was a picture of a couple in love, except the man in the picture was my husband.

"Imogen, you've been separated for four months now. He's found someone else. He's happy."

He did look happy. Their faces were framed in broad grins. And their hair was windswept. There was an ocean in the background and some mountains as well. They were on a vacation, somewhere. And then I noticed her fingers, her long, slender fingers painted with bright red nail polish. She was wearing an eternity ring. The one he'd given me and then, had asked for it back, the last day he'd stayed in the apartment, saying it was a family heirloom. I didn't protest. I'd taken it off my finger and given it to him, nearly throwing it at his face. And now I know why he'd asked for it. To present it to someone he'd been dating. While he was still married to me.

"I know what you're thinking," Marsha's voice whispered from behind my ears. "But he swore to me that he did not have an affair. That he'd met her after he'd left you."

There was a long, dead silence in the musty room.

"He asked me for the ring the day he left me. That was four months ago. In the photo, it's not winter. They're wearing summer clothes. And the bloody ring is on her fucking finger."

Marsha didn't have anything to say, she looked away.

"You knew about this all along, didn't you, Marsha?

"Don't accuse me, Imogen! I'm not part of any of this. He mentioned that he'd met somebody else, he'd mentioned that he was leaving you—he told me you knew everything."

"Well, I didn't, clearly. I didn't know that he'd met another woman. Don't you think it's a crucial detail to share with someone when you're leaving them after twenty years. And more importantly, when you're pinning the blame for the dissolution of the marriage on that person?"

I paused, and then said, "When you're demanding most of the money that was made during that marriage for your own keepsake, leaving me nearly penniless, these details matter. Infidelity. He was having an affair, Marsha."

"My son would never do that!" Marsha shouted at me.

"Proof is in the photograph. Look at it. It's late summer at best, and she's wearing the ring. This was around the time he left me. Unless your precious son met somebody and proposed to them the same day, I don't think that's how it went down. Don't you agree?" I spat out sarcastically. The room was spinning, and I was filled with an intensity of hurt and betrayal I'd only read about in novels, but this was happening to me. In my life. Not a movie or a fiction novel. The pain kept stabbing at me from the inside in waves. And I felt the tears well up.

"I'm not going to let him get away with this," I finally said, trying hard to hide the utter humiliation. "People have affairs. It happens all the time. And Devlin can leave me for another woman. That happens too. But he's not going to get away with demanding everything in the divorce. And what he put me through, blaming me for the end of the marriage, saying things like he'd lost respect for me when all along he was philandering. I won't let him get away with that. It's abuse. He might have been the principal breadwinner in the family, but I raised our children. I was a damn good mom! I gave my heart and soul to this marriage, to this union. And I worked when I could. Your son is a liar and a betrayer."

"Don't you dare come into my house and call him these things!" cried Marsha, looking frantic.

"Well, the lawyer's going to be interested to see this photograph," I said and rushed over to pick it up from the credenza.

"Give it back!" she shouted, rushing over to me, and grabbing it from my hands. But I wouldn't let go, my strength proving to be too powerful for the aging woman.

"I won't let you have it!" Marsha screamed.

"It's too late," I said, and I pushed her, a little more forcefully than I should have. She stumbled backward but didn't fall down. And with the photo firmly in my hand. I grabbed my coat and purse and left the apartment, slamming the door behind me.

The adrenaline was racing through my veins as I ran down the stairs and out into the cold winter air. But I was warm inside, a cauldron of heat, tears freely flowing down my cheeks. I thought of the last few months. Of my life together with Devlin. The countless dinners, quiet evenings, vacations, love-making, escapades with the children. And then later, how he'd turned on me and blamed me, finding fault in everything: that I was lazy, unambitious, narrow in my thinking. *Uninspiring*, was the word he'd used. And all the while, it was because he'd met another woman, younger and prettier. God, she couldn't have been over thirty. Blond and buxom and blue-eyed. What a cliché.

Suddenly, my mind went to Michael and back to Killin. When we were young and in love, how pure and innocent that had been. Filled with hope and promise and a sense of the unconditional. Look at what my life has become. I couldn't take these thoughts anymore. I stomped down Fifty-Second Street, until I hit Park Avenue. There, I turned left and walked down a couple of blocks until I reached the nearest bar. I went inside and ordered myself a stiff vodka. Neat. I sat at the counter and plotted my future course of action. I was not going to let him get away with this. After a few stiff drinks, I'd decided it was time to go home. I reached into my wallet, and that's when I felt the hard edges of the business card in my hand. I fished out the piece of paper and saw the name of Detective Max Murphy of the NYPD, Special Crimes Unit, printed reassuringly at the center.

I was going to get myself a good lawyer and fight this out. I was tired of being pushed around. And if I was going to get a good lawyer, I needed money, all the money I could scrape together. Lubricated by the alcohol, I took out my cell phone and unsteadily, dialed the numbers on the card. The phone rang a couple of times and then a familiar voice picked up.

"Hi, this is Detective Max Murphy speaking."

"Hello, Detective," I said, sounding unsure. "This is Imogen McLelland. I hope you recall, we met a few nights ago. Along with Eoin at the bistro. From Killin … "

"Of course, I remember you, Imogen with the beautiful name," he said warmly. "How can I help?"

"I was thinking about that offer you'd made. About me doing some consulting work for the NYPD, Special Crimes Unit ... "

"So, you're interested?" he reiterated.

"Yes. I think that I could be of service to you. I mean, if you're still interested."

"I sure am," he said, sounding intrigued.

"Except, I have a bunch of questions. I mean, how would this go down? How would it look to your fellow colleagues? I can't announce the fact that I'm a faerie."

"No, of course not. I don't know if you know this, but the NYPD has been known, especially in the past, to have called in psychics to help them in their investigative work, believe it or not."

"You're serious?" I said, bemused.

"I kid you not ... So, I was thinking we could introduce you as one."

"A psychic?"

"An intuitive person who has a sixth sense about people," he sugar-coated it.

"I didn't know these kinds of things happened in the NYPD, but yes, I suppose that could work."

"We don't do it often these days, what with all the technology, and we don't advertise it, but in cases where we're desperate, we sometimes do call in such people. And then, there's also the matter that it helps reassure the families that we're doing everything we can. But you have real skills Imogen, you really could help us. That is the only reason I'm offering this to you."

"Oh, Max, these 'skills' as you put it, are so rusty, I haven't gone to that part of my mind in years. Decades."

"Like you said, I'm sure it'll come back. You have nothing to lose, right?"

"You're wrong," I said. "I have everything to lose. My home, my money, my family, my children, everything is at stake. Because of my bastard husband."

"Oh dear, I see things have gotten worse on the home front," said Max, sympathetically.

I didn't know how much to share, but then again, I was looking for a job.

"Yes, I just had the pleasant misadventure of finding out that he'd been cheating on me, which is why he precipitated this divorce."

"Oh, Imogen, I'm so sorry."

"Yeah, well, I'm not going to take this lying down, I'm going to need money to hire a good lawyer. I guess I'm offering you my services."

"Great. That's fantastic to know," Max said. "Let me work out the details, and I'll send some paperwork over to you. You'd just need to sign and return it to me, and then, when we need your services, we'll give you a call. Between the two of us, I suspect you're going to be getting a lot of calls pretty soon. There seems to be a crime wave in the city after a long time. And of course, there's the Central Park Murders. Well, it's wonderful to have you on board, Imogen. I've got to rush now. There's a robbery afoot. And someone's been shot. It never stops, here!"

"Well, I'd better let you go, then," I said. "Thank you so much, Max, I really appreciate this."

"You're welcome. Goodbye."

And with that, the phone call was over. I had a new job, just like that. I was well aware that I'd negotiated myself into a job while I was under the influence. And you could call that liquid courage, but I was really glad in retrospect that I'd done it. I looked out the frosted windows of the bar. I could see the shimmering lights of the city and the vehicles, going up and down the roads and avenues. I could hear music out on the streets and the noise of the taxis and buses. I was allowing a part of myself that I had buried deep within to come to the surface again, after decades. And I was scared. Was it still even buried within me? I had made promises to help based on an instinct, so to speak, a power I'd possessed and that I hadn't used in such a long time. Would I know how to retrieve it? Would it still be the same? And so, I closed my eyes and let myself think about my Faerie nature. I delved deep into that part of my brain that harbored those powers.

But all it brought back was a bunch of nostalgia. I thought of my home in beautiful Scotland. The rolling hillsides that led down to the village of Killin. The river. The bridge where my beloved

Michael had taken his last steps. I thought of the wildflowers and the rain. I thought of my mother. My poor mother. Sick and ailing with cancer. I immediately shut out that particular thought.

At that very moment, disturbing me from the reverie I was immersed in, came a phone call. I'd saved the number so I recognized the name. I picked up the call.

"Hello, Eoin."

"Hi there, Imogen. I hope I'm not disturbing you."

"No, no, not at all. I'm not up to much. Where are you?"

"I'm on my way to the airport. I'm heading back to Scotland. I just wanted to check in on you to see if you'd come any closer to making a decision about coming home to see your mother."

I bristled at his forthrightness. I felt that part of me shut down again.

"I need some time to think about it," I said with finality. "I'll keep you posted. It was nice having met you."

There was a very long silence on the other end of the line.

"Of course. You must do what you must. I hope things resolve on the personal front for you."

"Actually, on that note, I decided to take up the job with the NYPD. I just spoke to Detective Max."

There was another long pause. "Well, I guess that means you won't be coming to Killin anytime soon."

"I don't know how it's all going to play out, Eoin," I said, defeated. "All I know is that I need to make some money soon, so my husband doesn't take everything away from me and sail off into the sunset with his beautiful young girlfriend. I just found out that he's been cheating on me."

"I'm really so sorry to hear of this," Eoin said, his voice low.

"I'll sort this out. And in the meantime … I'll give mum a call. It would be really good to hear her voice after all this time."

"Yes. You should do that," Eoin said. "I've left her details for you, as you know. She'll be so happy to hear from you."

With that, Eoin bid goodbye and hung up the phone.

My mother. She was the one person in the world for whom I had no words. There were no quantifiable means to calculate my love for her. But the only thing that exceeded the love I felt for her was the guilt of having abandoned her two decades ago, and the shame that crept up from that event had prevented me from ever being in touch. We do these things as humans, or faeries. Cruel things. When the intensity of feeling is so deep, we tend to avoid the matter entirely. And that's what I'd done for twenty years.

I fell in love and got married and had children and worked and made a new life, all the while keeping it entirely separate from my mother. Why I did this, I can't completely explain. I know it makes me sound like a monster. A selfish, unfeeling monster. Maybe I am. All I knew back then, as a young girl, was that I was incapable of processing having my mother in my life, and also, moving on and beginning in a new one in faraway America, knowing I was leaving her all alone to deal with a dangerous and violent husband.

But now, the two worlds were colliding, and I had to find a way to navigate it, or else I would never see my mother again. She was dying; my precious mother was dying. My heart ached.

Although I'd settled my tab, I turned to the bartender and gestured to him that I wanted another drink. He silently obliged. Yes, I had to tackle the mistakes of my past. But in order to do that, I had to confront my present. And that meant dealing with Devlin and his diabolical plans. Maybe all of this was karma for my behavior, I thought to myself, flippantly, as I gulped down the drink. I would not go silently into the night.

5

WHEN OUR CHILDREN ARE STRESSED, we are stressed. The next few days flew by in a blur as my kids were facing their fall term exams. This involved them calling me up in a panic at all hours and crying to me about deadlines and submissions and how they were behind in the preparation for their exams. You really feel their pain. I had submission deadlines of my own for the Manhattan Times. And I threw myself into my work, trying to keep myself busy in my apartment. I needed time to simmer, and I needed time to let things sink in. The last several years of my life had ended up being an illusion. Devlin was not the person I'd thought him to be.

He had always had his character flaws, but the one thing that'd made me fall madly in love with him was the one thing that I'd assumed had stayed pristine. His loyalty. His inner decency. This had enabled me to put up with his mood swings and, at times, sullen and difficult behavior. But everything was predicated on the assumption that he loved me deeply. I never questioned that. We had watched our children grow from babies to infants to young children and then, to young adults. We'd seen the trials and tribulations they'd faced. And we'd shared in their joys and sorrows.

Justin had wanted to become a doctor. He was smart and driven and did exceptionally well in school. When he gained admission into Yale University, we were overjoyed. He didn't receive a scholarship, but that was okay. His father would cover the costs. He would study pre-med, minoring in English literature. And the world was at his feet. I wish I could tell you it'd felt bittersweet seeing my own child go down the path of realizing his dreams of medical school when I couldn't follow my own ambitions on that front, but the truth was, I'd just felt happy for him.

In him, I saw my own potential that hadn't been realized come to some sort of denouement. Alexis had proven to be more difficult in trying to settle down professionally. Every week it was a new thing. For a period of time, she'd wanted to be a fashion photographer. And then, when taking selfies became a little bit too easy, she'd decided she wanted to study journalism. This had been her last fantasy, and I encouraged it, given my own experience in the field. She was good with words and was an inquisitive girl, and I knew she could make a name for herself in this field if she worked at it. But they were both so young, they had their whole lives ahead of them. Time to make mistakes and course-correct.

That's the thing about becoming middle-aged, you already are many things, and even if there still is enough time to readjust or even to begin again, you tend not to want to do that because the things that you have already become will inevitably shape the things that you will become. I knew then that I didn't want to be in a loveless marriage. Or worse yet, in an abusive one where I was constantly being put down. I knew then that my husband had cheated on me. And instead of owning up, had dumped the blame for the demise of our marriage squarely on my shoulders, like what cowards did.

When I thought of Devlin, I thought of two different people, and I couldn't reconcile myself into believing they were one and the same person. The mind can play tricks on you when it's late at night and you're lying in bed, sleepless, reflecting on your life. I was grateful when the phone rang. It was half-past eleven. But the gratitude immediately turned to alarm when I thought of my children. I scrambled to pick up the phone and turned the light on by the bedside

"Is everything okay? Hello? Who is this?" I asked, frazzled.

"Imogen, I'm so sorry to be calling you this late. It's Max, Detective Max. I'm sorry if I woke you up, but do you have a minute to speak?"

I was disoriented for a moment, then regrouped myself quickly.

"It's no problem, sure, I can talk."

"Sorry, again. Well, just to bring you up to date, it seems like we have some sort of a breakthrough in the case."

"What case?"

"You know, the case involving the brutal murders of the two women in Central Park?"

"Oh," I said.

"We've arrested a man, if you can call him that. We'd been receiving tips from locals in the area between Forty-Second and Fiftieth, along Fifth Avenue. That there was a bedraggled man with unkempt matted hair and filthy appearance who'd threatened passersby. And then, it actually happened. It seems he's ended up biting a young woman jogger right when she was about to enter the park. It wasn't a severe injury, but it got us thinking. The bodies we'd found had been riddled with bite marks. The coroner now confirms that these are indeed human bites. Given the savage nature in which the bodies were ripped apart, and the fact that this crime couldn't have been committed by an animal, as the victims were first bludgeoned on their heads to death, we felt it imperative to bring this man into questioning."

"I see, and what is it that you want me to do?"

"Imogen, we want you to come in and work your magic. We want you to talk to him and see if you can make any sense of it. Sense of him. If he is indeed the culprit for these crimes, I mean, could you get an idea? With your Faerie intuition or whatever? Would you be able to do this tomorrow morning? That's why I've called you this late. I wanted to catch you before you'd committed yourself to other plans."

I paused for a second and then answered.

"Yes. I can do this."

"I must warn you, this man seems dangerous. He will be handcuffed and chained, of course, and an officer will be present. But he almost behaves like a beast. He doesn't talk, all he does is snarl and growl. He's filthy, unkempt, with matted hair and dirty teeth. We think he's mentally unstable."

"But do you have any other proof apart from that of his appearance and his alleged attack on the jogger? Did someone witness the attack?"

"No, but we're trying to match the bite marks on the bodies of the victims with his dental impression. If we can get one, that is. The thing is, he doesn't allow us to go anywhere near him. We probably will have to sedate him to get the information we need. We have him arrested for attacking the jogger. We're working hard to get all the information we need before he lawyers up with a public defender."

"I can make it in at eight tomorrow morning if that's not too soon?"

"No, the earlier the better, in fact."

"But if he doesn't talk?"

"Well, that's precisely why we want you to come in. Eoin told me a little bit about how faeries empathize and can sense other people's natures. Perhaps if you're in a room with him, even if he doesn't speak, you can get an idea about his nature; whether he's capable of committing these horrific acts. I mean, I don't know how it works, but I do know the power of the Faeries to be true. I've witnessed it first-hand."

"And you've told your colleagues that I'm a psychic?"

Max grunted a little, and then he said, "I'll be informing them tomorrow morning. I know I haven't initiated the paperwork yet, but it should be smoothed over, quickly enough. I'm trusted by the Crime Scene Unit. They'll allow me this leeway. The most important thing is that we get you in a room with this man as soon as possible, before the lawyer arrives."

"Okay," I said. "But I must warn you, I'm very rusty."

"Yes, yes, Imogen. I know you've not done this for a while. But this is your chance to shine," Detective Max said flippantly.

I nervously laughed on the phone and then bid him goodbye and hung up. I wasn't even sure if this work was worth it. I didn't know what they were going to pay me. All I knew was that I had to fight for my life, now. And every dollar counted. If something good came of my interactions with this person, this bedraggled, unwell man, perhaps that will translate to a decent, steady income from the NYPD. Who would have thought? After years of working on and off as a journalist in Manhattan, I would end up moonlighting as a faerie, using the skills that I'd vowed I would never allow to surface again.

Everything seemed up in the air as I lay in bed and looked out the window and saw the night sky, glittering with stars. I thought of my own homeland. It would be early morning in Killin, back in Scotland. The farmers would be up and heading to their barns and fields, tending to the cattle and sheep. High Street would still be quiet, desolate and cold, waiting for the impending bustle of the day around the corner. And my mother would be in her large house all by herself. Slowly getting out of bed and making herself a cup of tea, her bones aching and her body slowly withering away under the weight of the disease that had overtaken her.

Yes, everything in my life seemed up in the air, and the only way I could hold on to any sense of sanity was to allow the feelings to wash over me. I had to believe that there was a larger plan, that everything would add up if I just took one step ahead at a time. That my professional and personal life would settle down. But at some point, I would take the flight out to Scotland. When that would be, was anyone's guess. But first, I needed rest.

But unfortunately, the night mixed itself in my dreams in the worst way.

I was being chased by some hideous evil in the death hours of the night, across the darkened fields. It was freezing cold and I was young again. My feet were bare and the air damp with moisture, as I raced across the plains in the Scottish countryside, being chased in the dark by something so sinister, I couldn't stop to turn and see what it was, lest I lose it all. My life.

The moonlight guided me past trees and shrubbery, and scratches were chafed onto my skin as I ran with all my might. It was right behind me, its presence growing closer and closer. And then, when the evil was almost upon me, and I let out a frightening scream that echoed across the plains, I would wake up.

My body was drenched in sweat and my bed damp with moisture. As I sat up in my bed and caught my breath, pearls of sweat beading their way down between my breasts, I realized finally that something was wrong. Really wrong. It was one thing to be having these terrible nightmares, but the vividness of it all was unbearable. And the night sweats. The sheets were completely drenched, and I wearily removed them and put on new bedding.

Were my dreams trying to tell me something? Was I on the cusp of some terrible danger that I was unaware of or hurtling towards. I felt the locket dangling from the chain on my chest, rubbing it with my fingers. It reassured me with cold comfort that I was there, I was alive, and I'd lived through a terrible nightmare. That was all.

6

THE POLICE PRECINCT WAS ABUZZ with activity even at eight as I made my way over to the receptionist.

"Hi there, I'm here to see Detective Max Murphy. I'm expected. My name is Imogen McLelland."

"And this is concerning?" she asked me, staring down the edges of her spectacles.

"It's a matter of police work. I'm not sure I'm supposed to discuss it."

She gauged me for a long while and then said, "Hold on," picking up the telephone and making a call.

"Alright, I'll send her your way," she said, and down the receiver.

"Max is expecting you. Please make your way to the third floor and walk to the end of the aisle. His desk is on the right."

"Thank you," I said, and made my way to the elevator. All the while, I kept thinking to myself: What a ludicrous idea. I was presenting myself as a psychic. There was no such thing! Charlatans pretending to know something about the world of the supernatural and the arcane, when really, they were just regular human beings trying to make a quick buck. I wondered how many innocent lives had been exploited, how many false hopes had been raised, with their claims and theories?

I reached the third floor and walked to the end of the corridor and there was Max, staring at me, smiling warmly.

"Imogen, so glad you could make it."

Next to him was a tall, well-built man with dark, wavy hair and a grisly beard.

"This is my partner, detective Alberto Romeiro."

"Hi, nice to meet you," he said, looking at me quizzically. I immediately felt self-conscious.

"Is everything alright?" I asked, extending my hand in greeting.

"Psychic, eh? Can you tell me what I'm thinking right now?" asked Alberto, facetiously.

"I don't think ... it doesn't work that way," I said, staring at my feet. I felt like a fraud. I had to keep reminding myself that I really did possess special abilities, just none that I could talk about without coming across as insane. Not that psychic sounded particularly normal in any case.

"Well, we could use all the help we can get on this case, and apparently Detective Max thinks the world of you. Maybe you are just a very intuitive person. Who knows?"

"An intuitive person on whom we're spending precious departmental money," came a booming voice from behind. I swung around to see an imposing man, tall and with a silver beard. I was soon introduced to the chief of the department, Detective Cooper. His words hit at the core of me, and I felt ashamed to be there.

The serious look on his face immediately morphed into one of levity, as he said, "Relax, I'm just giving you a hard time. Don't worry about me. I completely trust this gentleman here in the grand scheme of things," he said, pointing to Max, "and if he feels you've got a gift, by golly, you must have something. Anyway, I'll let you folks get down to it. You have a difficult customer on hand," he said, referring to the man in custody.

Max and Alberto ushered me into a separate room and closed the door.

"So, were the teeth marks a match?" I asked Max.

"He won't let us go near him, but we will sedate him. Soon. Maybe you can convince him."

"You say he won't even talk?" I asked.

"No, he just growls like an animal. He looks like a wolf, with hair growing out of his ears and well, generally, he's hairy all over. And filthy," Alberto added, flailing his arms about as he described him, looking disgusted.

"It's hard to go anywhere near him, he smells so bad. He probably hasn't bathed in months."

"I suspect he must be mentally unstable," I said. Though I had no expertise in the matter, it just seemed a possible explanation.

"Yes, that's what we all suspect, but mentally unstable or not, he might be responsible for these murders, and if so, needs to undergo the due process of law.

"And he will be handcuffed?" I asked again, looking nervous.

"Yes, Imogen, he will be handcuffed and chained to the table. Plus, there will be a policeman, watching over things. You're totally safe."

"So when do I meet him?"

"Right away, if you're ready. He's here, in the precinct."

"Alright then," I said, taking a deep breath, "let's do this."

I followed Detective Max and Detective Alberto further down the corridor to a room at the end where I was asked to wait. It had two chairs and a metal table in between, and nothing much else. There were cameras at the corners of the ceiling to record the proceedings. A policeman stood at the entrance. Max and Alberto disappeared. I sat in the cold room, on the edge of my chair and thought about the ethics of holding people culpable who were seriously mentally ill. I was not an expert on this subject, of course, but something about it tugged at my heartstrings. Suddenly, I remembered the bodies torn asunder, and the bloody, bludgeoning of their heads, and any empathy I'd felt quickly disappeared.

Some people just aren't fit to be in society, I thought to myself. Fifteen minutes passed, and I started getting restless. I had an assignment due later that day for the Manhattan Times. It had been an unusually busy week for me with work, and I was happy about this. But it meant I had to get home and start typing away at the computer in order to meet the six o'clock deadline. Suddenly, the door opened and a stench so awful that I gagged wafted into the room. The smell gave way to Max and Alberto, ushering in, who could best be described as a beastly man. He was barely recognizable as a human and had the most menacing grin on his face. He had piercing blue eyes and pitch-black hair that had been matted by dust and leaves and twigs, and it had grown to shoulder length. His hands had been chained together. There was an excess of hair everywhere, sprouting out of his ears, overgrown on his arms and even from his nostrils. He surveyed the room for a moment and then he looked directly at me with an intensity that shook me to my core.

He was shuffled forward and made to sit down, forcefully, on the chair facing me. He was then shackled to the table.

"Imogen, I hope you can talk to him and get him to open up and tell us a little about himself. There's nothing more to say, really. We'll leave you two alone. There's nothing to be afraid of. There's a policeman here in the room, right beside you." A tall man stood guard. Even as both the detectives left the room, I could barely hear the words out of the mouths of the detectives. I could hardly sense the presence of the tall policeman standing guard. I wasn't even aware of the awful stench that was emanating from across the table, anymore. All I could do was stare directly back into the limpid pools that were the eyes of this beast-man, sitting across the table. As certain as the next breath of air that I was going to take, I knew something upon seeing this man. I knew it with certainty. I knew it the way you know the sun rises every day and that the seasons change. And recognized it in the way I recognized my love for my children. It was an instinctual recognition that needed no words, but it was omniscient. It pervaded the room, and as far as I was concerned, it was the only thing that was there: the realization that I was in the presence of someone supernatural. His presence reached out to the very core of me, that intrinsic part of my being that held my Faerie nature. He stared back at me, not menacingly, but with an intensity that foreshadowed a recognition between us. I was sure he'd recognized there was something different about me too. Well, that's what I'd imagined, anyway. My heart started racing and my mind was alive with curiosity. A kindred spirit!

"Hello. My name is Imogen. I've been asked to talk to you to find out a little bit about who you are. What's your name?" I asked.

There was no response. Just the staring. I persevered, completely transfixed.

"Is there anything you'd like to tell me?"

Again, there was no response.

"I'm here to help you, but only if you open up and share something about yourself. I can help exonerate you and get you out of this situation you find yourself in."

For an interminably long moment, the foul-smelling, hairy man stared at me. And then, most unexpectedly, he leaned forward, resting his elbows on the table, opened his mouth to reveal his yellowed teeth, and with parted lips, said, "I'm Brendan."

7

I LOVE MY CHILDREN, BUT this was the first time in nearly two decades of being a mother to these incredible beings that I'd brought into the world that I'd mixed feelings about their presence in my home. They were driving me nuts. Alexis was lying languorously on the couch, distracted by her phone and all the while telling me about the wonderful Samantha in her life. Samantha. Devlin's new girlfriend, and the woman who'd, for all practical purposes, stolen my husband away from me.

Of course, Alexis didn't know that.

"She's so awesome, mum. She's kind and friendly, and she lets me borrow her clothes. Oh, and she's so fashionable! You'd think that being a doctor, she wouldn't be fun, but she takes me all over with her friends, and we drink wine, and gossip about boys, and I discuss my dreams with her. It's almost like having a second mum. I mean, you get what I'm saying, right?"

Justin quickly interrupted, looking at the stunned and brooding expression on my face.

"She's just kidding, mum. No one can replace you. What's the matter with you, Lexie?" he chided his sister, even as he flipped through the channels on the television. Alexis' words sunk like the ballast of a ship to the bottom of my heart. I knew there was no point in trying to correct her because if that's what she was feeling, then that was that. So, I decided to be immature instead.

"Why is she drinking wine with you? She shouldn't be encouraging you to be drinking alcohol. You're not even of legal age."

"Oh, mum," Alexis, rolled her eyes. "I'm in college! Everyone drinks in college. It's not like I'm guzzling down bottles of alcohol," she said, glancing knowingly toward the liquor cabinet on the credenza, arranged meticulously with bottles of all sorts of spirits, toward the side of the living room in which we were seated.

"It's just a glass of wine or two, when we have lunch or dinner."

"So, how often do you meet her? Spend time with this Samantha?" I asked, trying to sound cool.

"Oh, I don't know. I see her when I go to Dad's on the weekends, to spend time with him."

"But that's only been a few weekends since you started college, right?" I prodded, trying to piece together my daughter's vague and cavalier words.

"She's in community college, mum. She can waste all the time she wants," Justin snorted in condescension.

"I am so sick of you acting superior, Justin," Alexis retorted. "We can't all go to Yale. Besides, I'm doing Mum and Dad a favor by not spending hundreds of thousands of their dollars on an expensive education."

"Oh, is that why you're going to community college?" Justin took her on.

"I actually, quite like it. The classes I'm taking are interesting. And the professor in journalism is really good. I'm not a snob like you, Justin."

As my kids argued and bantered with each other, I stared blankly at the television screen even as the channels were being flipped. I felt this great sense of foreboding. A feeling that things were slipping away from me. I couldn't discuss my troubles with my children, and that made me feel very alone.

Samantha. How Alexis praised her. Suddenly, a thought occurred to me.

"How long have you been hanging out with Samantha?" I asked my daughter. "When did you meet her?"

I tried to ask this nonchalantly while staring at the television screen, but my ears were pricked.

"Why, mum, are you jealous?" Alexis suggested, a hint of mischievousness in her eyes.

"Lexie!" shouted Justin. "Don't be a jerk."

"Oh, I don't know." Again, the vagueness. "A couple of months. Two, I think."

"And you're already best friends?"

"She's really nice. Dad seems very happy. Besides, she's more in tune with our generation."

At that, I turned and stared at my daughter, horrified.

"What do you mean?"

"Well, mum, she's a lot younger than you."

"Oh, that's just fantastic," I said, at a loss for words.

"I know this is difficult for your mum."

"You don't know anything, Alexis," I said.

"Well, I know it must be difficult for you. But try and understand that Dad is happy. Wouldn't you want that for Dad? I really wish you started dating again."

"Sometimes, it alarms me, Lexie," I responded with an even keel. "How you don't think about the fact that I was in a twenty-year marriage before you speak. It ended four months ago. And you're already telling me to move on. That Dad is happy with another woman. Sometimes I wish you'd listen to your own words and realize that you're not the most empathetic of people. The times when I need you to be anyway," I said, feeling hot tears well up in my eyes which I quickly wiped away before they fully bloomed in my eyes.

There was a long, awkward pause in the room. Justin finally said, "She's right, Lexie. You can be really insensitive, sometimes. I mean, I understand you're an airhead. But even airheads need to show sensitivity."

"Mum, I didn't mean to upset you," Alexis finally responded, hinting at a sliver of cognizance. "Justin, go to hell."

This was the beginning of another lengthy argument between my kids, but I'd tuned out. I'd come to a decision. I didn't have it in my heart to tell my children that their wonderful father had been sleeping around even before the marriage had ended. It would have broken their hearts.

So, I decided I would leave this aspect, this crucial aspect of infidelity, outside of the divorce proceedings, going forward. I'd set up a meeting up with Lancaster and Associates, the law firm I'd decided upon that would represent me. I would tell them the whole story, but I would ask them to keep this matter out of the courts. I didn't want to hurt my children's impression of their dad. They were sentient beings, at least Justin was, and were all grown up and could come to conclusions on their own. They may have not shown their true feelings to me on the divorce, but the pain would've been there; the confusion they must have been feeling, and which was probably why Alexis was lashing out at me in the manner that she was with her insensitivity.

I was sure my children were going through a lot on account of the separation and impending divorce. Justin was more withdrawn about his feelings. Maybe this was because he was a boy and felt that it was a sign of weakness to show vulnerability, retrograde as that may sound. But I suspected it had affected him deeply. But his grades were still up and he sounded cheerful enough.

My daughter, Alexis, was another matter. Any thought that went through her head would come tumbling out of her mouth. In a way, this was good, because it meant I knew exactly what she was feeling, or so I'd imagined, but as the events of the afternoon had just revealed, it could also mean opening myself up for a world of incredibly cutting and hurtful conversations.

"Anyway, mum," Justin interrupted my train of thought. "I think you'll feel better about the whole thing when you meet her tomorrow at dinner. Samantha," he said, looking at me.

"I'm not thrilled about the fact that I have to share Christmas dinner with your dad and his new girlfriend," I blurted out and instantly regretted it, but surely it was understandable under the circumstances.

"I mean, it's okay," I said quickly. "It's what needs to be done. Besides, it's high time I met the Samantha. Since you're spending so much time with her and she's so wonderful and all," I said, staring at my daughter who pretended not to hear my laced words.

"Oh, I don't know if the two of you will get along," Alexis continued, staring at her phone. Justin blanched and stared at his sister inquisitively.

"I don't think that's going to be the case, mum. Besides, it's understandable if you didn't get along or if there was tension, given the circumstances," Justin added.

"I just think you should give her a chance," Alexis said. "She has nothing but wonderful things to say about you."

I looked at my daughter, incredulously.

"How could she possibly have wonderful things to say about me? She's never even met me, Alexis. It sounds fake."

"Why do you have to be such a pill about everything? She's been really nice and gracious. She's told us she's not there to replace you," Alexis continued on her mindless tirade.

"You sound like a twelve-year-old," Justin said to Alexis. "We're grown adults. We're kind of in charge of our own lives now, Alexis. Maybe you need to grow up."

I closed my eyes and leaned back onto the sofa. I thought of the long weekend that lay ahead of me and the prospect of having Christmas dinner with the young doctor-girlfriend of my husband. My prevalent thoughts all proved to be a source of discontentment and sadness, one that I couldn't shake off, and I wanted to stop thinking about this subject. I let my mind wander. I found it settling on the strange, unkempt man that I'd encountered the day before at the police precinct.

Brendan had revealed his name, but then when I'd tried to get him to speak more, he'd clammed up and said nothing else. I'd persisted, but he wouldn't open up anymore. But he had said his name. His first name. It'd come out from the depths of trauma that were the layers of his mind. The connection that I'd felt, I wondered if it had something to do with him opening up a little. The connection I could only feel with another supernatural being, a magical being.

In my life, most of those supernatural beings had been faeries back in Scotland. But this hairy beast of a man, Brendan, was no faerie. I didn't sense that kind of connection. He was something else. Of a different supernatural vein. It had filled me with excitement and a sense of expectation, sentiments I'd hadn't experienced in a while, life having whittled me down in the recent past to a middle-aged woman on the brink of divorce from an unfaithful husband. What a tired and tried trope of an existence. But, every time Alexis and Justin started talking about Samantha and Devlin, I clung to this new, unfamiliar and exciting train of thought. And it lifted me up out of the gloom. It was a puzzle to be solved. A mystery to unravel. And at the center of that mystery lay a man who'd literally emerged out of the woods after twenty years, and in a battle to save his already embattled life.

I'd already figured out a vital piece—a crucial piece. And that was why I'd been brought in, in the first place, by Detective Max. I'd realized, deep in my soul, that Brendan was not the murderer. He was not the perpetrator of these vicious crimes in Central Park. He couldn't be. I was an empath. It was my gift. And I could sense no evil in his presence. He had a clean spirit. I was willing to bet my fledgling moonlighting career as a faerie detective that Brendan was innocent. Of this, I was nearly certain. How I was going to convince the detectives of this, was entirely a different matter.

I was a psychic, remember? So, I suppose I could've proffered that I thought he was innocent because of the feelings he inspired within me. But the truth was, the Faerie way of being, the magic we possessed was something far more real and visceral—it was woven into our bones and into our beings. I probably still cannot find the right words to express what that magic is, but I'd trusted it with all my heart when I was a child. I knew I possessed it. And it was that part of me that Brendan had reached out to and with which he had resonated. And though he'd refused to share anything more with me, I was determined to keep trying until the man would open up. If he was innocent, and this was something of which I was almost certain, he needed to be exonerated of this crime.

I was shaken out of my reverie with the sound of Justin and Alexis arguing, once more, over something ridiculous. I'd had enough.

"Kids, I'm going to step out for a while, I need some fresh air. I'm probably going to the grocery store. Can I pick up anything for you?" I offered.

"A pack of cigarettes," Justin said.

"I'm not going to buy you smokes, Justin. It's a disgusting habit."

"How about a bottle of wine, then," Alexis asked, half in jest.

"Great, I'm bringing up a bunch of addicts," I said, as I grabbed my coat and purse and bid them goodbye as I walked out of the apartment. I was hugely grateful for the respite. I loved my children more than anything in the world, but somebody had to be the adult in the relationship. That meant I couldn't tell them anything and had to put up with everything. I had to be stoic. I'm sure this is not unusual in parenthood, I'm nothing special, but it still didn't make it any less real, happening to me.

Infidelity. The crumbling of a twenty-year marriage. Lies and deception. I'd taken the elevator down and then stepped out of the building straight into the cold, wafting air. Directly across from our fancy apartment on Fifth Avenue was Central Park. A park that contained many sinister secrets from the recent past. Again, that sense of danger and evil lurked and then swept over me. It was close to me. It rattled me and I looked around, but there were just pedestrians walking about, and the taxis and cars whizzing up and down the avenue. Something or someone dreadful had walked through the park's wooded regions, recently. They had ripped apart these young women, these innocent young women.

I took my cell phone out of my winter coat pocket and called Detective Max.

"Max, hi, this is Imogen. Hope I'm not interrupting something?"

"Oh, hi Imogen. Not at all. Go ahead."

"Yeah, I was just curious to know if Brendan has said anything? Since yesterday?"

"Nope. He's been really quiet. In fact, so quiet that I'm finding it hard to believe that that man had actually opened his mouth and whispered his name."

"You know he did, Max. It's on tape."

"Well, it's not much to go on, but we're running it through the databases. Unfortunately, it's the Christmas weekend, so we're low on staff and high on crime."

"Criminals don't take a break for the holidays?" I offered, rather facetiously.

"I'm afraid not." I could hear him grinning at the other end of the line.

"Well, I'm sorry I won't be available this weekend as I have family duties to tend to, with my children back from university for the break."

And then I volunteered something, the motivation for which I still don't understand. "And then, there's the unpleasant business of having Christmas dinner with my husband and the woman with whom he'd cheated. The kids don't know this. It's a mess."

I immediately regretted oversharing.

"Oh, I'm sorry about this, Imogen," came Max's patient reply.

What more could he say?

"That's gotta be tough, having dinner with the woman who's ripped your family apart. I'd want to punch her in the face," he offered.

"Yeah, I actually kind of want to do that," I said, and laughed, nervously.

"Oh, my God, I was just kidding, Imogen. Now I'm worried!" Max said, and laughed.

"Don't worry, I'll be well in control," I offered. I knew I would. And my insurance policy was my children. I wouldn't do anything to traumatize them.

"Well, anyway, Max, I just wanted to check in about Brendan."

"If that's who he says he is," Max interjected.

"Yes, well, have a wonderful Christmas weekend, and I will be in touch on Monday, okay?" I said and hung up.

I turned left and walked down Fifth Avenue. Suddenly, I was overcome with a feeling that all of this, the street which housed my apartment, the home that I'd lived in for years, my life, that all of it had been ephemeral, and that it was winding down to an end. Whether this was good or bad, I couldn't say, but I knew in my heart that change was around the corner. And that I had to be strong and resilient and ready to face it.

8

IN RETROSPECT, I SHOULD HAVE KNOWN it was going to be an utterly unpleasant evening. I sensed it in my bones, felt it in my guts, and yet, I'd held onto some irrational wisp of hope that it would all go swimmingly well. Big mistake.

As I walked into the palatial apartment in the swanky new high-rise building on Madison Avenue and Fifty-Seventh Street, the feeling of foreboding that enveloped me almost instantly should've been enough to make me turn on my heels and run out of the building. But I had to endure that evening for my kids. And for saving face. I was drawn to that evening the way people are drawn to the site of a car accident—part-horror, part-curiosity—all laced with the frantic need to rectify something that had already, unfortunately, happened. I needed my lousy, soon-to-be ex-husband, to realize that he was not going to get away with everything.

With unaccountability. That he wasn't going to win, and that I'd had my dignity intact. And even though he was going to parade his new girlfriend in front of me, even though I'd have to bear witness to the burgeoning relationship between Samantha and my children, being played out right in front of me, I was determined not to let them have the last laugh. My reasons were complex for being there, but it was Christmas Eve, and I always spent them with my kids. My children deserved to have both their parents present.

What an apartment. With a vaulted ceiling in the foyer and steps leading off on one side to an upper floor, it felt like I'd walked into a European aristocrat's residence, not the hastily rented property of a cheating husband. What money could buy! There was marble all around, and it made my blood boil to see that my husband, who was trying to ensure that I was left with less than nothing in the impending divorce settlement, was splurging on this fancy apartment. Yes, he had worked for it. Devlin had risen up the ranks steadily, from almost nothing. He'd had an unhappy childhood in the Bronx, and this was his answer to it: a fervent need to prove to the world that he was different, unique. That he could rise to the challenges of a tough life and overcome them, no matter the odds. It had been a pivotal part of what had attracted me to him when I was young. His tenacity. But back then, I'd not seen that this need to prevail, to thrive no matter what, when left unhindered, could grow to unmanageable heights of hubris.

To be throwing his indomitable will to thrive and be happy in my face, nary a few months after we were separated, and to be hosting this dinner with his new girlfriend Samantha, had all been a bit too much, in retrospect, for my frazzled heart, at the time. Hindsight is twenty-twenty. My husband hadn't answered the doorbell. It was Samantha. Beautiful, blonde Samantha, perfectly proportionate and with a cherubic smile to go with her fine-featured face, welcomed my already racing heart.

"Hi! You must be Imogen. So lovely to finally meet you. Please come on in. Devlin is upstairs getting ready. He'll be down in a minute."

This immediately upset me, that the woman was acting like this was her home already. She'd barely known my husband for ... well, that was the thing. I couldn't say how long, but it had certainly overlapped with my marriage. I could barely muster up a smile as I said my hellos and quietly entered the spacious apartment. Alexis and Justin were already there, squabbling over something or the other in the living room that the foyer led into, and into which I was ushered.

"Oh, hey, Mum. I see you've met Samantha," Lexie said nonchalantly as if this were the most normal situation in the world.

I was completely on edge but was determined not to show it. I sat down gingerly, at the edge of the sofa next to my children and waited patiently for my husband to come down from the upper floor. Samantha was like a thorny, unpleasant presence in the room, and I tried hard not to make eye contact with her, but when she thought I wasn't looking, I did take a good look. She was beyond beautiful. She was stunning. And she was a pediatrician. She had to be a doctor, didn't she? And she was so young! Late twenties? Early thirties? I felt my heart sinking. Well, whoever she was, she didn't think twice about getting involved with a married man. I clung on to that morsel of information in my mind as if it were the only thing real in a world of hurtful apparitions, spinning into my vision in that apartment. I needed something to hold onto, anything, to reassure me that she wasn't superior.

"Oh, hey, Im," I heard Devlin's voice from the background as he came into the living room. Handsome as ever, and clearly fresh from the shower, with little beads of post-shows sweat clinging to his forehead, I stared at him agog. I felt a lurching sensation in my gut. How could he have done this to me?

"Hello," I said icily.

"Good. I'm glad we're all here. It's good that we all got together. Well, what do you think of the place?" Devlin asked.

"It's fancy," I said, abruptly.

"Well, what's the point in making money if you don't spend it? Right, kids?" Devlin asked his children, jauntily.

Justin was trying hard not to get drawn into the tension in the room and was focusing on flipping channels on the television, as always.

"So, Imogen, Devlin tells me you're a wonderful writer. That you write for the Manhattan Times? I've picked up that magazine from the stands on occasion. It's a fun read," Samantha offered.

Supercilious. I hated her already.

"Actually, mum wanted to be a doctor, just like you, Samantha. When she was in Scotland. But she decided to hop on a plane and come on over to America instead and try her luck."

The words reverberated in my ears and stung my soul. I couldn't believe my own daughter was letting me down like this. Where had I gone wrong with her?

"Oh, really? I didn't know this," Samantha said, looking pleased as if she'd won a silent victory over me.

"Well, that was a long time ago. I don't even think about it anymore," I said, dismissively.

"I can hear traces of that accent. Scottish, right?"

"Yes." My responses were monosyllabic.

"That's so exotic. I've hardly had time to travel in my life, being so busy with medical school at first and then with my training and practice. I guess there are trade-offs for everything," she said cavalierly.

"Can I get us all some drinks?" Samantha asked, looking around the room as if she were the hostess of this soiree. I stared at her with hostility.

"Yes, that would be good," I said. There was no way I was going to get through the evening without alcohol.

"Maria is cooking up a fantastic storm in the kitchen," Devlin offered, referring to his new hire, a personal chef. "Let me get my phone and play some music. Any requests, Im?" he asked. It was as if I was watching a pitch-perfect enactment of what would be counted as a normal festive occasion in any other family. Except this was not. The voices in my head grew louder and the anxiety increased.

"Nothing too loud," I said. I could hear my heartbeat thudding in my years. I did not feel good about this evening at all, and we were only a few minutes into the gathering.

Samantha returned with drinks for everyone. Red wine was decanted generously into all our glasses. And then she sat down next to Devlin and placed a hand gingerly on his thigh. I was beginning to get a reading of this woman. It was mixed. She clearly wanted to mark her territory, and yet, she was making an effort with me. She was trying to be polite. Just when I stopped to think that maybe, just maybe, my perspective on things, and of this person, was being colored by the circumstance, Samantha asked, "So, what area of medicine did you want to specialize in?"

I thought it was slightly cruel behavior, belaboring the point of a touchy subject that was done and dusted. It reeked of a desire to manipulate the conversation, just to illustrate that she was superior to me. But I had to answer. "Surgery. I want you to be a general surgeon."

"Oh, that's tough work. I knew early on I wasn't cut out for the surgical sciences," Samantha prattled. "I'd always wanted to be a pediatrician, and luckily I could become one. I just love kids. It always bothered me that I hadn't had children of my own."

The woman was barely thirty!

" ... but now, with Justin and Alexis, I feel like I have children of my own," she said triumphantly, staring at me all the while.

The evening was getting to be unbearable. I was extremely grateful for my son, Justin, at that moment, because he looked at me apologetically, and winked. This gave me strength, that one of my own kids could see how difficult and strange this was for me, and empathized with me. That someone there could understand how painful all of this was for me. Painfully unbearable. I just wasn't in the mood to make small talk. Luckily, Lexie opened her mouth and said something that offered the opportunity for a change in the topic of conversation. Some respite.

"What do you think about these awful murders in Central Park? Totally gory and gruesome, right, dad?"

"Oh, let's not talk about such unpleasant things, Lexie," Devlin pleaded. "It's too horrific to discuss."

"Can you believe it happened so close to where Mum lives?"

That's right, it was the home I'd shared with my husband. Not anymore. It was my house, now. Well, at least for now.

"Let's change the subject," Devlin insisted.

"One can't be too careful these days," I said, as my thoughts fleetingly drifted to Brendan. But they were quickly interrupted by some soft jazz music that Devlin started playing on his phone, picked up by the speakers. The living room was softly inundated with soothing music, but it was too mild a stimulus to comfort my thorny internal world. I couldn't help looking at Samantha. I couldn't help focusing on the fact that my husband had lied and cheated on me, and I couldn't help but feel bitter toward the farce that was being enacted that evening as if everything was okay. A flimsy bandage over an open wound. I was in a combative mood, lubricated by the alcohol, and though I wasn't aware of it at the time, the evening was precariously balanced on the precipice of a carefully timed enactment, one of deception, and it was inevitable for it to come unraveling. I was never one for artifice and duplicity. They'd always inspired a low tolerance in me.

When it came time for dinner, Samantha curiously juxtaposed herself next to me. Her friendly demeanor continued, and the banter flowed around the table with me sitting silently, and staring at the elaborate spread. I drifted in and out of the conversation, feeling invisible and falling silent as a mouse.

"Do you remember that antique shop we went to in Michigan, Devlin? When was it?" Samantha said.

Suddenly, Devlin looked alarmed. "Uh, yes, Sam. Has anyone tried the roast beef? Maria has really outdone herself."

"Well, I was just telling Lexie about the beautiful bracelet that I'd found at that antique shop. I told her she must go there. What a lovely day that was, Devlin, warm and sunny," she said.

"Do you mind passing the gravy?" Devlin interrupted, looking very uncomfortable. And that was when I snapped. My husband, my as-yet-to-be-divorced husband was sharply indicating to his girlfriend with his stare, to keep quiet. But I'd had enough.

"So, when was this trip?" I blurted out and asked, turning to face Samantha on my left. Suddenly, there was pin-drop silence in the room, and the clinking of porcelain and cutlery and wine glasses fell silent.

"I beg your pardon?" Samantha asked, carefully.

"When was this trip to Michigan? With the warm and sunny weather?"

"Oh. Oh, I don't know, a couple of ... a while back." It was dawning on Samantha that she'd overplayed her hand.

"How long ago?" I asked, again.

"Imogen, this really isn't the place to be discussing this," Devlin began.

"Shut up!" I screamed. Suddenly, the charade was over.

"When was the trip, Samantha?"

"It's none of your business, really," she responded, to my utter shock. She really was horrid, underneath that sugary sweet exterior.

"Oh, I most definitely think it is my business. A couple of months ago, perhaps? That was when I was still married to my husband. It was sunny in Michigan, eh? That wasn't any time recently, clearly."

No one spoke. There was total silence. I'd had enough.

"Or are you too much of a coward to speak the truth? Samantha?" I prodded.

"It was this summer," she finally said spitefully, turning to face me. There wasn't a hint of remorse in her eyes.

I turned to look at Devlin accusingly. "You'd said you'd gone for a conference, Devlin. To Ann Arbor." Devlin stared at the meat on his plate.

"Say something!" I screamed. "How long was the affair going on?"

Again, my question was met with silence.

"If you don't speak honestly, Devlin, I swear this is going to become a serious issue in the divorce."

"Keep your voice down." Most shockingly, the words came from Samantha.

I turned around in horror to stare at her.

"Excuse me?" I whispered, barely being able to contain my rage.

"Don't talk to my mother like that," Justin spoke up. He was in my corner and suddenly, Samantha, decided to back-track on her aggressive stance.

"There's no need to shout," she said. "Mistakes were made. But let's face it, you were ... Devlin was in a dead-end marriage. He was unhappy. He'd wanted to move on for some time, he told me. The affair, while perhaps not in the best of taste, brought to an end an unhappy marriage. Now, both of you can move on."

I couldn't believe this young woman, sitting next to me, and justifying the breaking up of my marriage, as if it were just a piece of paper, a contract, that'd been signed twenty years ago, and that she'd taken upon herself to render null and void.

"Don't comment on my marriage, you know nothing about a twenty-year association with someone," I said, feeling the tears well up.

"Look, I know Devlin was unhappy. And now, he's happy with me," she said, smiling at him, artificially. "Life is too precious and too short to live in an unfulfilled and compromised manner. There are some of us who want more from life than just settling. Devlin and I are on the same page."

Devlin looked aghast and just kept staring meekly at the table. The gloves were off with her last comments.

"Yes, speaking of moving on ... " I said. "You seem very comfortable in this spacious, expensive apartment."

Samantha stared at me, and almost spat the words in my direction.

"I'm a doctor, a pediatrician, I make a ton of money. I'm not a social climber. But if that's what you're implying, if anything, that would be a description that would better fit you."

I wanted to take the fork in my hand and stab her for saying that.

"Will the two of you stop this!" Lexie interrupted, screaming.

In the middle of all the rising tensions, I'd forgotten to observe my daughter. She had tears streaming down her face. I immediately felt regret, terrible regret for having brought all of this up at the table, but what was I to do? I was only human. But Justin had had enough.

"Mum, we don't need to listen to this woman disparage you. My mother is not a gold digger," he said, staring at Samantha with disgust. "And if you ever say something like that about my mother again ... "

"Justin, don't you dare threaten Samantha," Devlin interrupted.

"You're defending her? A woman you've known for a few months, over your own wife?" Justin was shaking with anger and hurt. It was as if he'd finally come upon realizations that he'd been trying hard to avoid accepting. There were no more pretenses now.

"No," Devlin said, sounding flustered. "I'm just saying things are not always what they seem and kids tend to get confused about these things. It's complicated, Justin."

"There's nothing complicated here, Dad," Justin said flatly, and with a precocity I hadn't seen from him before. "You fucked another woman. And now, you're trying to flaunt that in mum's face while taking everything away from her."

"Justin!" screamed Devlin. "Don't you dare talk to me like that, ever again."

I just sat there, feeling helpless and numb, at this point. I picked up my glass of wine and gulped down every last dreg of it. Then, I stared at Devlin and said, "I'm done talking to your girlfriend. I asked you a simple question: how long have you been cheating on me?"

"Devlin, don't answer that," Samantha interjected. "You've said enough. The divorce proceedings, the lawyers, the legal stuff ... "

"Shut up," I said to her, dismissively. And for once, Samantha listened.

Devlin took a deep breath, wiped his face with the napkin, laid it on the table, and then looked me squarely in the face.

"I'm really sorry to have put you in this position, Im. But the affair has been going on for over a year."

I couldn't believe what I'd heard. The year that had passed, the holidays, the quiet evenings, the vacations, the drudgery, the intimacy. Suddenly, it all played in my mind like a time-lapse camera. I realized it was all an illusion, a grand deception. He was sleeping with someone else the whole time, developing another relationship, making plans that didn't involve me.

"If you were so unhappy, why didn't you tell me?" I asked.

"Oh," Devlin said, looking flustered, momentarily. "I wasn't that unhappy. It'd just become time to move on."

I was flabbergasted, I didn't know what to make of this anymore. Samantha sat brooding, next to me, staring at the napkin on her lap, clearly unhappy that Devlin appeared less eager to participate in my vilification. Lexie was openly wailing. And Justin had got up to get his coat.

"Mum, we're leaving. Let's go," he said. I was so grateful for my son at that moment. And for the fecklessness of my daughter, I could and would forgive her. She was still young and unformed. And after all, it was my mistake to have brought up the ugliness in front of my children. Mistakes had been made all around that table that fateful night. Horrible, scarring mistakes. But the truth was finally out. I'd felt hurt and bitterness over a man I'd clearly never completely understood before. For all my secret faerie powers, Devlin, the man I'd shared a life with over the last twenty years, had proven to be a complete stranger to me. Or maybe, he'd changed, and I just hadn't noticed it. I'd taken him for granted, thinking he would always be a part of me.

In that moment, I also realized that people can switch off from others for no reason at all. Even if everything was okay. That the human heart could be really fickle. I got up on my feet, and suddenly felt very unsteady. I realized I'd had a little too much to drink.

"Justin, it's good you're going home with your mother. She's not fit to walk home alone. Not when she's drunk."

And that was that. Whatever little softness my husband had shown me a second ago had vanished and had been replaced with the cruelty of those words. He was like a chameleon, switching his colors back and forth, unsure of his allegiance to those around him, and unsure of his own true nature. He was wanting. It wasn't me. The feelings in me surged, and before I had control over them, I'd picked up the wine bottle at the center of the table, uncorked it, went over to my husband, and emptied it over his head.

"To let me down by sleeping with another woman, after twenty years of marriage, is deplorable, Devlin," I said, even as he sprung from his chair and tried to wipe the alcohol off his clothes. Samantha was screaming at me, but I didn't listen to a word. I continued: "But to let me down and call me a drunk in front of our own children because I've come into your home on Christmas Eve, and I've had to witness the charade of my yet-to-be divorced husband playing house with the woman he's cheated on me with, and as a result, ended up having a bit too much to drink. To be labeled like this by the father of my kids, and it's something which you have, by the way, even tried to use against me in legal proceedings ... it's beyond words. It's deplorable."

I turned around to face my children. "Yes, kids. He's the one who cheated on me, and yet he wants to use my alleged drinking habit against me so he can squeeze out as much as he can from the divorce settlement. This is your father."

"Stop it! All of you!" Justin screamed. "Look at Alexis! She's a mess. Let's just go home. This evening is over," he said. I looked at my son and realized shamefully, that he was the only one who was acting anything like an adult that evening. He took me gently by the elbow as I grabbed my coat and purse and we went into the foyer. Maria was standing in the background looking flustered. Before we left, I turned around to look at an apartment I never wanted to see the insides of, again. The alcohol was coursing through my veins. I made eye contact with my husband, and shared a look, one that seemed to ask him why? It was a voiceless thought, but I hoped he understood what I was trying to convey. Then, I turned around, held my son firmly by the arm, and before I left, faced Alexis and asked, "Are you coming, Lexie?"

I wish I could say I was surprised by her response, but her words finally confirmed many subversive thoughts that had been surfacing in my mind in the recent past, thoughts that I'd tried to suppress for I'd not wanted to face them.

"No," she said, through her tears. "I think I'll stay with Dad tonight."

"You've got to be kidding," Justin said, disgusted.

"Nevermind," I said, feeling guilty for my outburst.

"You're a real shithole, you know that?" Justin said to his sister, even as Lexie's wailing reached a crescendo. She ran into her father's arms. I couldn't take any more of this drama, unfolding like a badly enacted play. I turned around swiftly and left the apartment, Justin following protectively behind. I pressed the elevator button, and we stood there silently, on the fifty-second floor, waiting for the whirring sound of the machinery to reach our level so that we could leave this mess behind. I felt numb and impassive. And then, my son said, "Mum, I'm so sorry, I had no idea. I didn't know that Dad was having an affair. I thought he'd met Samantha after you'd broken up.

I ... I can't believe that he would do such a thing to you, to us. I'm so sorry," he said.

And, in an instant, I ran into his arms and hugged him deeply. The pretense was over. I started crying. And for the first time in a very, very long time, I felt a sense of relief and a feeling of solace, that I was finally being understood by someone that I'd loved. I felt overwhelming gratitude.

The nightmare happened again, only this time it was more vivid.

I was running across the fields at night in Scotland, under the moonlight, with the cold entering my body and enveloping me with a chill that was heightened by the imminent danger I was in. I was being chased. Hunted down. By what or whom, I couldn't say, not daring to turn around. I was overcome with visceral fear, the likes of which I'd never experienced before. I was running as fast as I could, my lungs on fire and my thighs burning with heat, but it was catching up to me. The demon in my dreams. It was almost upon me. And just when I turned around, screaming in terror, almost in its clasp, I woke up.

I was gasping for air and immediately reached for the glass of water on the side table. My heart was racing and my body was utterly drenched with sweat. I had ruined the bedsheets which were soaked with sweat as well, and my pillow covers were drenched, too. This couldn't be normal. Again and again, I kept having these dreams, and unlike anything I'd ever dreamt before, so real and almost like a premonition. Or was it a glance into my past? That it was catching up to me? What was chasing me? And why did I wake up just when it was about to reveal itself to me in a deathly clasp?

I looked at my soaked sheets and muttered a curse underneath my breath. I couldn't keep doing this. Changing linen in the middle of the night wasn't ideal either. I made up my mind that I would see my general physician and get a prescription for a light sleeping aid. I'd had enough of this nonsense.

9

THE WEEKEND PASSED BY IN A BLUR. Alexis refused to pick up my phone calls, and Justin hovered around me protectively. I mostly stayed indoors, flipping television channels by myself and thinking about the year that lay ahead. My heart was heavy and my mind was a blur with the traumas of all that had happened on Christmas Eve. I couldn't believe I'd let things get so out of control. I was ashamed of myself, but at the same time fomenting with the knowledge that Devlin had morphed into this human being that I could barely recognize. That he would put me down in front of this woman he'd known only for a short time. And that he would allow her to talk to me in that manner in front of the mother of his children. It was unacceptable.

Alexis' behavior. It was like a thorn in my heart, one that I just couldn't wedge out and one that was buried deep inside. I couldn't understand it. Had she changed so much in the few months that she'd been in college? Or had she always been like this? A slightly reckless and unfeeling young woman? Where were my Faerie instincts? I was to assist the police with a criminal investigation, my work pegged on my supernatural abilities, and yet, they'd completely failed me when it came to understanding my own loved ones. This had happened before. With my father, Mark, back in Scotland. I'd always known he was a small-hearted man, and that it was in his biological make-up to be cruel, but to be revealed as a murderer in the end? And why hadn't I sensed that Michael was in mortal danger? And from a man with whom I shared blood and a home! My mind was all over the place.

I thought of the heritage that both my children had unwittingly inherited. But I quickly tried to bury the thought. I didn't want to go there. I was a half-blood. Part Seelie Court and part Unseelie Court in my Faerie heritage. How much of this had my children inherited? My precious daughter? I had the wickedness coursing through my own veins, and yet, I'd fought my whole life, to try and be a good person. Or so I'd thought, anyway. My mind went to my mother, and then I realized, perhaps I was a mix of good and bad after all, in the way I'd treated her. Everything was churning in my head, and I had to shut it down, so I watched television blindly. And slept in late. I found comfort in focusing on what I was eagerly anticipating: Monday morning. Another encounter with the infamous Brendan. I wanted something, anything different, and on a positive note with which to end the year. I was eager for it to be over. The year my marriage ended. The year my husband called me a drunk in front of my children. And the year I seemed to have lost Alexis.

Brendan had yet to speak to the detectives, but I'd come up with certain ploys to try to get him to open up if indeed, it was reticence that was keeping him quiet. Maybe he's suffered some sort of psychological or worse, neurological damage? But, I was excited by the fact that I was in the presence of someone supernatural, a kindred spirit, in that sense. I was motivated by the fact that I could sense there was no evil in him, I was almost certain of that. And I really wanted to do a stellar job on my first assignment, and, if possible, exonerate an honest and innocent man in the process.

On Monday morning, I got out of bed early. I had that sinking feeling in my chest, the one that I always got when Justin headed back to college. The empty-nest syndrome never really goes away, it's just something you just learn to get used to, or so I'd imagined. I had, sadly, not. I made him his favorite breakfast, eggs benedict, and fussed over him as he packed his belongings and headed to the door. A cab had been called.

"I'm going to miss you," I said to my only son, giving him a deep hug, tears welling up in my eyes.

"Mum, I know you're going through a difficult time," Justin said. "But I know how strong you are. You're the one who's being wronged. You. And if you need any assistance with the divorce proceedings ... you know, testimony from your kids or something like that, well, I can't speak for that daughter of yours, but I will support you. I am on your side," he said, holding me tightly. I could see he was struggling to leave me behind in what he perceived was, and not entirely without merit, a trying and volatile situation. I was extremely reassured and deeply moved by these kind words from my beautiful son.

"I'm just so proud of you, Justin," I said, smiling at him, and ruffling his curly red hair. I'd brought up a good boy. "But, I'm not going to drag you and Alexis into these divorce proceedings to the best of my ability."

"I want to help, Mum," he protested, looking concerned.

"I know. And it really means so much that you would say that to me, son," I said, holding his hands in mine. "But this is a battle I need to wage on my own. Don't worry. Your mum can take care of herself," I said, with as much reassurance as I could muster. With that, I kissed him on his cheek and he turned around and left.

In an attempt to not allow the silence in the apartment to grow to a screeching and overwhelming crescendo, I quickly got into the shower and then hurriedly dressed so I could head to the police precinct. I made it there just before nine. Max was already there, and he told me that Brendan was in the holding room.

"You're in for quite a treat this morning, Im," Max said wryly. I raised my eyebrows and looked at him expectantly.

"What happened? Did he speak? Did he say something? You've figured out who he is?"

"No, no, nothing of the sort. He's been as quiet as a winter's night."

"Then, what is it?" I asked, growing concerned.

"You'll see for yourself," Max said with a grin, and took me down the corridor, like before, to the interview room. Max partially opened the door and I could see Detective Alberto Romeiro sitting on a chair in front of a metal table, casually munching an apple. He seemed utterly nonchalant. But when the door was fully swung open, I saw someone who instinctively took my breath away.

On the other side of the table was a strikingly handsome man, with alabaster skin, black hair, and blue eyes. He had chiseled features, and I could make out he had an athlete's body, with long limbs and a lean torso. I was completely flustered for a moment. And then, I stopped dead in my tracks. Max could see the confusion on my face and chuckled to himself.

"Yes. Lo and behold. The mysterious Brendan, primped and showered and shaved," Max said. I tried to cover the look of complete astonishment on my face, but in retrospect, I realize it was a bit too late for that. I tried to look nonplussed, and smiled at Brendan, even as I went inside, and over to the side where the detectives were sitting down. My heart was racing for some reason.

"Good to see you too, this morning, Imogen," Alberto said, pointedly.

"Oh, I'm sorry, Alberto. Good morning," I said, my cheeks flushing at my rudeness. And the fact that I'd felt everyone in the room could read my thoughts.

"I'm having moments of existential crisis here," he continued.

When I looked at Alberto inquisitively, he said, "I don't know what we're doing here with this man, anymore. He won't speak. Not a word. We just sit in an interview room and stare at him hoping he'll open his mouth and utter words in our direction. It's ridiculous. We should be at the crime scene, with the others, Max. Combing it for more clues." When Max stared at him, silently, Alberto continued, "Maybe, he doesn't speak English."

"Maybe," Max mirrored his words. I could see that Max was thinking through the scenario, planning his next moves.

I'd found it amusing that they were talking about a person who was sitting right there, watching him as if he were not in the room, but a fictitious character that they were discussing. Like from a movie. I couldn't take my eyes off, Brendan. He was in his mid-forties and could have been any person in Manhattan. A corporate lawyer. A Wall Street tycoon. A doctor. An accountant. Nothing about his appearance suggested the years of unusual trauma he'd clearly endured. Worse yet, he kept staring at me. He wouldn't take his eyes off of me. It made me flush. My cheeks went red, and I looked away.

"Anyway," Alberto continued, "we should be hearing any moment, from the forensics department, about the bite marks. That

106

should give us some definitive answers about our Brendan, here," he said, right to Brendan, as if he weren't in the room, again.

I found this insensitive. But, why was I feeling protective toward this person? Supernatural being though he may have been, I wasn't sure of his innocence. Not yet. I needed to talk to him. But with each passing moment in that room, with his eyes fixated on me, I was increasingly certain that I was in the presence of good energy. A clean spirit. How I was to prove this, and how I was to convince a police force of this, were seemingly insurmountable tasks that lay ahead of me. How would everything add up? How could I conduct my work and come to conclusions without it raising eyebrows? I knew I had Max on my side, and in the know of my Faerie heritage, but I'd still need to convince him of Brendan's decency. I was racing ten steps ahead and had to force myself to stop with the conjecturing. I took a deep breath and closed my eyes, momentarily.

The door rattled open and a sergeant walked in with papers in his hand. He looked completely agog as he stared at Brendan.

"Yes?" Detective Max asked, impatiently.

"You've got to take a look at this," he said, handing over the papers to Max and Alberto. The pages rustled in an otherwise silent room, and I could see the expressions on the faces of the two detectives go completely ashen. They looked at each other in amazement, as if they'd encountered a ghost. My heart started racing again, with anxiety and apprehension. And then, they turned to face Brendan, staring at him, intently.

"What's happened?" I asked. I couldn't help it, my curiosity had reached a peak.

After an interminable silence in the room, Max opened his mouth and said, "Brendan Connor. You're Brendan Connor."

I felt flustered for a moment. I knew this was a big moment. That they seemed to have identified the man at the center of the storm and sitting in front of them. The name sounded vaguely familiar to me, too. Brendan continued to stare only at me, and without any expression on his face.

"Jesus. Good Lord Almighty! Is this confirmed?" he asked the sergeant again, who'd carried the papers into the room. The man nodded, silently. "It's a forensic match from the missing person's report filed twenty years ago."

"What's going on?" I asked again, feeling unheard.

"Imogen," Max began, hesitantly, "this gentleman here, sitting so silently, is Brendan Connor. Do you remember the case of the missing millionaire's son, from two decades ago? The boy who'd disappeared from a mental health facility? And he was never to be found again, presumed dead?"

To my surprise, I realized I did remember the case. I remembered it because it was all over the news when I'd just come over to America from Scotland.

"Wait, you probably weren't even here at that time, right?" Max said while continuing to stare at Brendan like he was an exhibit in a museum.

108

"I'd just arrived," I said, quietly. "I remember the case. It was splashed across the news. It was everywhere," I said, looking at Brendan with pathos. I could have sworn at that moment that there was a flicker of recognition in Brendan's eyes, as he stared at me. That there was some movement behind those big, blue eyes. I really felt I could reach out to him, that I could make a connection if given a chance.

"This is unbelievable," Max continued. "A high-profile person being found after nearly twenty years, right in the heart of Manhattan. In Central Park.

Max was having trouble digesting the facts, clearly in amazement.

"And now, presumed to be the infamous serial killer, bludgeoning women to death and then tearing up their lifeless bodies," Alberto added, laconically.

We all stared at Brendan expectantly, but he didn't say anything.

"Brendan, for god's sake, this is your chance to open your mouth and say something. We're going to notify your parents, now that you've been found," Max continued, expectantly, hoping to see some kind of emotion or response from Brendan, at the mention of his parents.

But Brendan just kept staring at me all the while, even as the detectives looked at me, quizzically. And then they left the room, leaving the sergeant with us. There was a deafening moment of silence as the two of us stared at each other. I felt as if he could see right into the part of me that was strongly attracted to this beautiful man. I hadn't quite processed my thoughts or feelings yet and was reacting viscerally, and in the moment, and it embarrassed me that I felt he could see right through it all. So, I tried to cover up the turmoil that'd overtaken me inside by turning my gaze away and looking at the clock on the wall.

"I remember your case," I finally said to Brendan. "I'd just arrived from Scotland. I'm from Scotland, by the way," I said. He just kept staring. "It was all over the news, as Detective Max said. And, after a few weeks, it was assumed that you'd died. Because, you know, you had escaped from a ... "

I felt uncomfortable saying the words out loud, " ... a mental health facility. And were assumed to be a threat to yourself. I'm sorry, I'm rambling," I said. Shut up, woman! I said to myself, silently.

And then he said it. It came out of nowhere: "I'm not mentally ill."

The words smoothly rolled off his tongue, as if he'd been talking normally all the while before dropping that bomb. But, the truth was, for a man who'd said nothing for days, those were indeed strange and telling words, in retrospect, to be the first to come out of his mouth.

I went rigid as I stared right back at him now, looking stunned.

"I'm going to get the detective," said the sergeant at the door. "Will you be okay?" he asked me. "The man is tethered."

"Oh, I'll be fine," I said.

Before I could open my mouth and ask Brendan anything further, the detectives, Max and Alberto, returned. The guard told them what had happened.

'So, he just spoke out loud," the sergeant apprised them.

"What? What did he say?" Max asked.

The guard looked uncertain and turned to face me.

"Brendan just told me that he was not mentally ill. That's it," I said, consternation lacing my voice and features.

Both the detectives looked completely confused and stared at me.

Max quickly turned his attention to Brendan and said, "Brendan, can you speak some more? Is there something you're trying to say? This is the time to talk!

And, much to their dismay, Brendan, again, went completely silent.

"Are you sure he spoke?"

"Yes," I said. The other detective concurred. "It's on tape, sir." I nodded my head.

"For crying out loud, Brendan, if you can speak, speak!" Alberto shouted impatiently at the man.

But Brendan's eyes turned stone cold, and he turned his gaze to the floor and stared. That was it. The detectives looked exasperated.

"Do you understand the implications of your words, Brendan? If you were mentally incapacitated or ill, when you committed those horrific acts, your lawyer could fight for a milder sentence for you. Get you less jail time. But if you're found guilty, and you swear that you're mentally whole ... it's not going to look good for you in court," Max persisted.

"Brendan, why did you say you're mentally fit? I can't believe I'm saying this, but you probably shouldn't go around saying that, given that you're accused of horrific murders. Given that you have a history of mental health issues, let's stick with that narrative until your rich lawyers arrive, alright?" Max said.

"Why are you on his side?" Alberto pulled Max aside, clearly irritated.

"I'm not on anyone's side," Max replied. "I'm just saying, the law does take into consideration mental illness."

"Why don't you gentlemen wait until his parents get you, before conjecturing on all these theories?" I offered, impatiently.

Alberto snapped at me. "You're hired for specific services, not for your opinions on how to conduct police procedures, Imogen, no offense."

"Hey, hey, there's no need to be rude to her," Max stepped in. And as the gentleman argued it out, the doors swung wide open and in came a suited lady, followed by an elderly couple. The couple stared at Brendan for a long moment in total silence. They soon had tears streaming down their face. The couple stood at the far side of the room and then, the older woman, exquisitely dressed and with her hair pulled tightly back, opened her mouth.

With a broken voice, she whispered Brendan's name. Brendan. The look on her face was pure agony and love. It was a look only a mother could have towards their child. A child they hadn't seen in twenty years. I turned to observe Brendan's face. There was definitely emotion there. His eyes glinted in the light.

"Brendan," she said again, moving a few feet closer toward him. The gap between them in the room seemed an interminable distance to cross, suddenly. "My darling son. It's you," she said, barely audibly, and burst out crying. She quickly crossed the room to her handsome son. The detectives tried to intervene.

"Ma'am, please stand back. He could be dangerous," Max warned, but she dismissed them, angrily.

"He's not dangerous, he's my son," she said, pushing them away, hastily, and then, rushing to embrace Brendan. He didn't resist. The father followed. For a few poignant moments, the elderly couple had their impassive son in their arms, and the detectives were not sure of what to do.

"There was no doubt that this was the billionaire, Frank Connor's son, Brendan. I couldn't bring myself to imagine how it would've felt, seeing your child you'd thought you'd lost forever, after all that time. And presumed dead. My heart went out to the parents.

"Brendan, sweetheart, where have you been? All these years?" the mother cried, as Frank Connor stood protectively next to his family. "What happened to you?" Nancy pressed.

Frank interjected, "Don't pressure him, Nancy. This is not the time for it."

"I want to know where my son was!" Nancy was getting hysterical. "Did someone take you? Were you held captive? Are you okay? Are you hurt?" The questions endlessly poured. And they were greeted with silence. But the expression on Brendan's face had visibly softened. He had emotion in his eyes and looked with love at his parents.

"Son, I'm so happy to see you," his father said with a quivering voice, trying to hold back the tears. "I'm so sorry," he continued. "I'm so sorry for the way I treated you. Perhaps we could have handled things differently back then, we didn't know what to do." This was a private moment.

I glanced suggestively at the detectives. And when I realized they weren't going to leave the room, I excused myself and stepped out. My mind was abuzz with questions. I was trying to piece together a puzzle, a story for which I did not have enough facts. If Brendan was supernatural, were his parents supernatural? But I hadn't sensed that in their presence. Not even a bit. But, maybe I was wrong. Maybe there was a deep family secret, buried underneath all the trauma. And if Brendan claimed he was not mentally ill, if he'd actually committed these horrific crimes on purpose, that would mean the end of Brendan. But then again, there were the conflicting feelings that I'd had, which had strongly suggested to me that he was completely innocent. Which brought me to the dreadful thought that if he was innocent, that meant the murderer was still out there. The serial killer. My heart was racing in my chest and my mind was raring to go in a million directions. I hadn't felt this alive in a really long time.

Straight across me, in the bustling, open office of the police station, detectives and secretaries and clerks were going about their day. Problem-solving crimes and murders and mysteries. It was part of their regular lives, getting to the bottom of things. But this was new for me. And the first case that had landed in my lap was one that involved supernatural beings. I had left behind my Faerie past when I'd come over to America, to the point that I'd hid it from my own family. There had been fleeting moments where I'd felt I'd been in the presence of supernatural beings in New York, but they were very few and far between. Twenty years had passed. And now, suddenly, in the span of a few weeks, I'd met Eoin and now, Brendan. It was as if my Faerie heritage was calling out to me again, and asking me to embrace it.

And, with the impending divorce, and the need for money looming, it almost seemed a necessity to delve into that way of life, again. I felt unprepared and rushed. And yet, I was excited to be embracing something different, as well. Conflicting feelings surged through me. My heritage: it was what had brought me to that moment. A part of me wanted to leave this new window of an opening and walk away. Go back to embracing a normal, human life, with all it's complexities and mundanely traumatic struggles. That would have been the moment to walk away. From Brendan and his mess.

But I knew I wasn't going to do that. The door to the interview room opened, and Max peaked out and signaled to me.

"Imogen, would you come in for a second?"

"Sure," I said, walking in, again. Again, Brendan stared at me with his searing gaze, and I felt like a fox in the headlights.

"Imogen, I want to introduce you to Nancy and Frank Connor. Brendan's parents."

They looked at me with a mixture of curiosity and hostility.

The suited lady, the brunette with the briefcase, looked at me sternly, and then turned her attention to Max.

"Detective, who's this and why is she here?"

"This is Imogen and she assists the NYPD, on and off, with certain important cases."

"In what capacity?" She asked, unimpressed.

Detective Max and Detective Alberto stared at each other, impishly. They realized there was no way to beat around the bush here, and spoke frankly.

"In some, high-profile cases, the NYPD consults with certain people who are intuitive. To help provide us with leads in cases in which we haven't been able to make much headway," Alberto began.

"She's a psychic," Max blurted out.

"What?" Frank Connor's expression darkened. "Are you joking?"

I felt the tension rise in my chest as I realized that I was an unwelcome presence.

"Detectives, is this some sort of prank?"

"No," replied Max with a steady voice.

"Yeah, well, there will be no psychic anymore, in this case," stated the lawyer. "I'll be representing Brendan from this moment on, and we don't have the leeway for such frivolousness. In this case, the stakes are high. Psychic, are you serious? That's one for the ages," she said, looking at me with disgust. "If you don't get rid of her this instant, I will be taking it up with your superiors and discussing it with the press."

Nancy Connor stared at me with steely disdain lacing her features. Frank didn't look impressed either. Finally, it was made abundantly clear to me what they'd thought of me. "Please ask her to leave. Right away," Frank said, authoritatively.

"Look, you may not approve of these methods, but she's the reason why Brendan opened his mouth and spoke, in the first place," Max volunteered, hurriedly.

"He spoke?" Nancy asked. Suddenly, the expression on her face completely changed from one of disapproval and condescension to that of confusion and vulnerability.

"Yes, just a few moments ago. When Brendan was alone in the room with Imogen and another cop. He volunteered some information."

"What did he say?" Frank asked, his voice urgent and booming.

Brendan was observing the fervid exchanges between the policemen and his parents and the lawyer, as if watching an unfolding play in a theatre, an objective viewer, with preternatural calm, and as if it weren't happening to him.

"We'll tell you in a moment what he said, Mister Connor, but the point is that it was Imogen's questioning and her presence that reassured Brendan enough to open his mouth and say something, who knows, probably after years! You may not value the services of people in her profession ... "

"They're charlatans," Frank said, sounding unconvinced.

"Easy, Mister Connor," said Max. "Whatever you think she may be, she could be a conduit to your son opening up. Wouldn't you want him to speak so you can find out what happened to him for all these years? Where he's been? What he's been up to? And his alleged involvement with these crimes?"

"My son had nothing to do with those awful murders in Central Park!" Nancy shrieked.

I wanted to open my mouth and say, yes, you're right about your son, but I couldn't.

"Nevertheless, we need to follow the due course of law," the lawyer interjected some normalcy to these extraordinary

118

proceedings. "You can't hold him on any charges that'll stick. The only 'crime' he's committed is being present in and around the park at the time of the murders!"

"Well, he tried to bite a couple of people. Pedestrians. And there were bite marks on those bodies ... "

"This is ridiculous. This is the 21st century. Did anybody file a formal complaint against Brendan for biting them? These are allegations. And regarding the murders, nothing you say can be backed up. Do you have forensic proof that his teeth match up with the bites on the bodies found?" asked the lawyer, impatiently.

"We're working on that."

"Well, until you can get those results, my client will be released immediately. You've held him long enough, baselessly. And now that we have identified him, incontrovertibly, as Frank and Nancy Connor's son, we'll be taking him home today. Now."

Max and Albert looked at each other and realized they'd lost this battle.

"Do you have any objections to us walking out of this precinct with Brendan now?" the lawyer persisted in a no-nonsense fashion.

"May I interject?" I opened my mouth at what seemed the most inopportune moment. There was complete silence in the room as all eyes turned toward me.

The couple looked at me disgustedly.

"I beg your pardon?" the lawyer goaded me on.

"Imogen, maybe this is not the moment to ... ?" Max started.

"If he's indeed to walk out of this precinct with you, and given that just a few moments ago I had made some headway with your son, perhaps I could be given a few moments alone with him before you take him home? He started to tell me that he wasn't mentally ill."

I'd had a sinking feeling in the pit of my stomach that the moment Brendan would be taken away and lawyered up by his rich parents, that that'd be the last I saw of him. And I didn't want that. Not just for reasons I couldn't process at that time, but because I wanted to help in exonerating him.

I was increasingly convinced Brendan was an innocent man. I'd had a connection with him, a secret connection. Being around his parents had convinced me there was nothing supernatural about them. But Brendan was special. I wanted some time alone with them. And I knew this was my moment to ask for that time.

"This is nonsense! We're not going to leave our son alone with this woman who ... " Frank began a tirade, but it was quickly interrupted

"Hold on, Frank," Nancy said. She looked at me sternly. She was a wiry woman and looked like she'd been through hell. I felt empathy for her, despite the harshness.

"You think you can get him to talk?" Nancy asked, looking solicitously at me, and then at her son.

"I'd like to try," I said.

"Did he really say he was not mentally ill?" Nancy persisted, looking at me.

120

"Yes," I replied simply.

She has tears welling up in her eyes.

"Oh, Frank, what if we made a horrible mistake twenty years ago?" she said.

"This is not the time to talk about these things, Nancy," Frank interrupted. And then he looked at me. "We're going to take our son home now. There are a lot of legalities to be pursued at this point. He's been accused of a terrible crime, one that Nancy and I know he couldn't have possibly committed. But we will allow you some time with him," he said, looking at me in resignation. The man was not used to having his decisions questioned, and it showed in his expression. "In a few days, not now."

"No, I'd like to talk to Imogen," Brendan said.

For a moment, there was total and utter silence. We'd forgotten to think of the man who was at the center of the storm as someone who could participate in these decisions. He'd almost become a symbolic presence, one who was to be debated and dealt with, not an actual, animated person, capable of contributing to the proceedings. His parents looked ashen as they heard the sound of their son's voice for the first time in twenty years.

"Brendan. You're speaking," Nancy whispered, holding her son's shoulder tightly. But he didn't look at his mother. He was staring at me. And then he looked away.

"I'll talk to Imogen alone now. And then I'll come home with you."

"And he speaks," Alberto muttered under his breath to Max, wryly.

My heart was racing. "Is this okay, Max?" I asked, barely being able to contain my excitement at Brendan's words.

Max nodded, after a pause. "Is this okay?" he asked the lawyer.

The lawyer conferred in whispers with the Connors and then turned back, and nodded in agreement. Clearly, she would've preferred to take Brenda home, immediately.

"We're going to have to record the proceedings," Max stated simply, looking at Brendan.

"Let this be done properly," the lawyer interjected. "This is not even a proper interview room. This is some sort of a holding cell. Please take him to a better room, with more light, and proper air conditioning. And for god's sake, give him something to eat."

"We've been taking good care of him," Alberto protested to the lawyer.

I suddenly realized an opportunity was presenting itself to me.

The lawyer continued. "The Connors want a few moments alone with their son, and then this lady can have some time with him. A few minutes best, after which we're going to take Brendan home with us. Okay?"

"Alright. Since this interview room is not good enough for you, let me go make arrangements for another. Get the cameras set up," Alberto said, walking out of the room. It really was a dingy room with a musty smell. It seemed like a room in which criminals had spent a lot of time. Not the place for a billionaire's son, judging by the expressions on Frank and Nancy Connor's faces. It certainly wasn't the type of room they were used to frequenting.

Max looked at me. "Imogen, let's wait outside while the Connors have a moment of privacy with their son."

I nodded, and we both stepped out. The lawyer remained in the room. Max turned to me and whispered, looking very serious. "Imogen, how you handle this is really important. I don't know how you did it, but please get him to open up to you. Once he goes home with the lawyer, it's going to be very difficult for us to have access to him, not unless we get more proof. At the end of the day, a crime has happened and it is our job as detectives, to get to the bottom of it. We have to stay on course and do a good job. However tragic the circumstances."

I nodded patiently. I could hear muffled voices coming from inside the room. No doubt the lawyer was tutoring Brendan on what to say and what not to say. I desperately needed a moment alone with Brendan before the cameras started rolling. I didn't know how I was going to make this happen, but I had to try. I had a plan in mind, to get him to open up. After a few minutes, the Connors and the lawyer emerged from the room.

"Well, he's not talking to us," Frank said. "I don't know what it is you have to do with this case, but if you could get him to open up, that's all I care about," he said, not even making eye contact. And then they walked away.

The lawyer remained behind. She stared at me squarely in the face and said, "Be careful. You're a lawsuit waiting to happen." With that, she walked away.

This was my moment. The detectives had yet to return to collect Brendan. I looked around, no one was looking at me. I snuck back into the room and shut the door behind me. I looked at Brendan and hurriedly said, "If anyone asks, I came here to retrieve a cell phone. I need you to hear me carefully, Brendan. I know you're innocent."

There was an interminably long silence in the room as he stared back at me with his mouth open.

"How?" he asked.

"I just do. Don't ask me anything about this when the interview happens in a couple of minutes. But know that I know you had nothing to do with these awful crimes. Hang in there. We'll get to the bottom of this."

With that, I left the room. My cheeks were flushed and my heart was pounding in my chest.

"What were you doing inside? Max asked, looking at me.

"Oh, I left my phone behind and went in to retrieve it. Sorry."

In a couple of minutes, Brendan and I were ushered into another room. It was much more spacious, with better ventilation and lights. And I could see the camera in corner of the room, recording everything. We sat across from each other, the detectives looked at us for a moment, and then left the room. Max turned around, just before closing the door, and said to me, "If you need anything, we'll be right outside. And, you can see, he's shackled. You've nothing to be worried about, okay?"

"I'm good," I said, with a smile.

I turned around to face Brendan. It was the first time that I was sitting directly opposite him. The supernatural aura that he radiated was so intense and dense, it felt omniscient. I had to remind myself that no one could sense its presence, except me. My thoughts instantly went to wondering about whether he sensed I was supernatural as well.

10

THE WEIGHT OF BRENDAN'S STARE was constantly on me and so, I had to look away as I sat across the table from him. We were silent for a couple of minutes. And then, I mustered up the courage to look him straight in the eyes and speak. I had to get this right.

"Brendan, why don't you tell me a little bit about where you've been the last twenty years? What happened? And if you can find the strength, about what happened in the park? If you'd witnessed anything?"

Brendan stared at me for a long moment with almost the hint of a smile on his face and then said, "I'm innocent of these crimes. I'd like to talk about what I've been accused of first, then I'll get to where I've been, and what I've been up to all these years."

"Okay," I said, listening patiently.

"I had nothing to do with the Central Park murders. But I'm connected to them. I'm guilty in some sense, as a result."

I felt a surge of alarm within me. Could I have been wrong in my reading of this supernatural being?

"I'm listening," I said.

"I've lived in the park for many years now. It's been my home. When you blend in with the trees and the bushes and the shrubs, nobody really notices you. Not if you want to stay hidden. The first murder, I didn't witness it. But I did come upon the body."

I felt a weight in my stomach sink to the very bottom. The words filled me with dreadful anticipation.

"You came upon the body," I repeated slowly.

"Yes. It was late at night. Was it a week ago? I don't know, I don't keep track of time," he said as if it were the most normal thing in the world.

"It was somewhere close to where I'd been, you know, living in the park. I'd heard a strange noise, as if someone was rushing through the shrubbery. This was strange as it was the middle of the night. After a while, I heard the sound of something crashing. I naturally went to investigate. And what I saw was ... it was something no person should witness. I can't imagine what that poor girl went through. It was like an animal that ripped her body apart."

"And you didn't report this to the authorities?" I asked gently.

"I've been missing for twenty years. I don't know how to explain this, I'm not like other people. I'm not normal, in some sense.

I can understand that people thought I was insane back then. Even though I know I'm not. I'm just different. It's hard for me to explain."

I knew exactly what he was referring to, and yet, I had no idea how to reassure him. I knew his secret."

"Go on," I said, looking at him with empathy. Somehow, I was hoping he'd remember that I did believe him and that it would reassure him, no matter how outlandish he ended up sounding.

"I probably should have called it in, I probably should have told someone. But I have not interacted with people, not really, in a really long time. And I was scared. I was scared that they'd accuse me of the murder. I just ... I just walked away. In fact, I was so disturbed by what I'd seen., all that blood, the torn limbs, that I shifted the locations of my ... "

"Your camp," I volunteered.

"Yes, my things, my few possessions, if you can call them that. The incident profoundly disturbed me. And frankly, ever since that night, I'd kept watch at night. To see if I'd notice anything or anyone unusual. Catch the perpetrator from repeating the act, you could say. I just had a sinking feeling it would happen again. But I failed in that, clearly. A couple of nights later, last week, I can't remember the date, sorry. My heart sank when I heard screaming in the woods, not too far from me. It must have been around two in the morning, maybe three. You're going to think even worse of me here because as I hurried over to where the sound was coming from, I saw I saw him.

The person who was murdering the young woman. It was a bright night, with a clear sky and a full moon.

"You saw him kill her?" I asked.

"Yes. It was horrific."

"Did you try to intervene?" I pressed.

There was a long, stony silence in the room.

"I couldn't," he finally said, staring at his feet.

"When you say you couldn't, Brendan, what do you mean by that? Were you afraid? I can understand if that is what you're saying. The man was dangerous."

"No, that's not what it was. I'm not someone to be afraid of many things."

"Then what was it?" I asked, dreading the way this conversation was going.

"I was ... preoccupied," he said, finally.

"The thing that makes me different," Brendan said, looking at me with a searing gaze, "it surfaces from time to time. At the most unexpected moments. Actually, around specific times of the month, but I can't say exactly when it will happen. But also, when my anxiety levels go up. Or I'm agitated. And when this thing happens, I am not in a position to deal with anyone else."

That was that. I looked at him completely crestfallen. I knew this was not going to go down well with the detectives of the NYPD. He sounded guilty. He'd been present, or close to both the murders, as he himself had clarified. And he claimed there was some sort of bizarre, vague, and inexplicable reason on account of which he couldn't intervene when he'd actually witnessed the second murder happening. And then, he failed to report both the crimes or seek help. It looked awful.

"Brendan, if you'd sought help, maybe the second girl could've been saved," I said.

"No," he said, bluntly, his eyes glazing over. "When I was finally able to go over to her, she'd been ripped apart. It was over."

"Brendan, what is this thing that you say that surfaces within you? From time to time?"

"I can't answer that question. All I can say is this: I'm innocent of all these crimes. I might not be a normal person, but I'm not a murderer. And, just to clarify, I did get a look at the face of the person who committed the crime, even though it was dark. Not sure if that's of interest to anyone, since all everybody seems to be hell-bent on doing is pinning this on me."

I know it sounded insane to an objective listener. Everything about Brendan's explanation reeked of guilt or at least, of a gross lack of accountability. He had flimsy, vague reasons. No reasons, in fact, except alluding to some mental health situation, perhaps. There was no way anybody else was going to buy it, but I did, for I knew something no one else did. That he really was not a normal person. And whatever he said that surfaces within him at trying moments, I knew he couldn't speak more of it because he really was alluding to his supernatural nature. He was trapped. I did believe him when he said he was not involved with the murders.

I couldn't quite make out, though, what exactly it was that prevented him from helping the girl in the second murder, at a moment of deathly crisis. I knew it was tied to his magical nature. He really was in a bind. And I felt helpless looking across the table and trying to silently reassure a man who clearly had a long battle ahead, to prove his innocence, and with no means of doing so unless he admitted to his magical nature. Which he could not naturally, and which was something I completely understood, given my own situation. My heart bled for him. I tried and composed myself, feeling the cameras on me.

"So, you saw the face of the murderer?"

"Yes, it's etched in stone in my mind. I would be able to identify him if I saw him again. I know everything that I say sounds implausible and strange and hard to believe. I know I sound strange and hard to believe, I know my life sounds unbelievable to most people. But this is all I can share right now."

Then, he looked at me blankly and said, "I've been advised by my lawyer not to say anything more. Well, I was advised not to say anything, period. But this is all I can share. I'm sorry."

"Why are you telling me these things, Brendan? Why me?" I asked him, not being able to help myself.

"It's just a feeling I have, that I can trust you. That you're someone who'd understand."

When he said this, I almost felt as if he was alluding to knowing something more than what other people knew about me. I couldn't be sure of this, though. Everything was functioning on gut instinct at that moment. My gut, Faerie instinct. But, my instincts were what I'd been called in for,

I was a faerie. Max knew that. This was my job. And I knew, with complete and utter certainty in my heart, that Brendan Connor, sitting in front of me, was completely innocent of the crime for which he'd been accused.

After the interview was wrapped up and we were leaving the room, Brendan glanced back at me one last time before exiting the precinct with his parents, both of whom seemed eager to get him out of there. Max came up to me and said one word: "Guilty."

I balked at him. "Imogen, please tell me you think he's guilty?" Max asked.

I looked at him flatly. "I know you know how I go about these things, Max. I know why I'm here, and what I've been entrusted with. So, I'm going to tell you something I need you to listen to carefully. I lowered my voice.

"I know this as sure as I know of the next breath of air I'm going to take. Brendan Connor is innocent."

"You've got to be kidding, Imogen," Max said, looking at me incredulously.

"No, I'm not," I reiterated my words. "He's innocent. I can read people like Brendan."

"What do you mean people like Brendan?" Max asked, looking at me, confused. I realized I'd let myself slip. I had to be careful.

"I can read him well, Brendan. That's all I meant," I corrected. "He's innocent. That's all I can say. It's my Faerie nature doing its thing. You called me in for this. It's your job to prove how, Max. But I would like to help you. Is there anything else you can share about Brendan with me? He was circumspect, about his past, about where he'd been. I mean, he cut me short before I really had the chance to ask him anything further."

"Yes, we spoke to his parents at length while you were talking to him. By all accounts, Brendan was a great kid. Very good at school. On the lacrosse team. A lot of sports, actually. He'd had a steady girlfriend right until a few months before he disappeared. Straight-A student. He was in NYU and was in his junior year when he seems to have had some sort of mental breakdown. His parents were convinced he was doing drugs and so was his flatmate. They'd held an intervention during which he disappeared. He ran out of the room, literally. This is what I am to understand. The next thing they knew, he was wandering around the outskirts of Central Park park, acting aggressive toward people and rambling strange things. His parents had him committed to a private psychiatric facility, convinced he was hooked on drugs. And then, like the papers said at the time, he disappeared one night. He escaped. That was the last they saw of this person, two decades ago."

After a long pause, Max bluntly said: "He's a drug addict, Imogen. He's had some serious brain damage, probably as a result. I mean, you heard him speak! He sounds insane!"

"That doesn't make him a murderer," I said, biting my tongue.

"No, but clearly he has mental health issues. And I'm not saying that that doesn't have a bearing upon his case. Which I'm sure will go forward now. Upon his arrest. But terrible murders have been committed, and if he's guilty of them, then he's guilty."

"He's not guilty," I said, looking Max straight in the face. That's all I could bring myself to say. Max knowing about my Faerie heritage was one thing, but it wasn't my place to be testing the limits of his tolerance of all things supernatural, by letting him in on what I'd come to believe of Brendan. Besides, it wasn't my secret to share. And how would I prove it?

I felt frustrated. I had complete empathy with Brendan. I knew how it felt like to hide a part of yourself, and to keep it constantly under check. Leading a double life.

"Is there any way you could be wrong, Imogen?" Max asked, looking at me sincerely. I was touched that he saw me with such credibility. I knew Max believed I believed in Brendan. That he'd had experience with and faith in the Faerie ways, thanks to Eoin.

"No," I said with finality. "There's just no way he did this. He saw the face of the murderer and yes, he seems strange and off, but wouldn't anyone who's lived in the woods for twenty years?" I asked.

"Strange case," Max said, all the while scratching his chin. "Oh, and there was one more thing. I was digging through Brendan's background, so I asked the Connors if there were any traumatic incidents Brendan might have had as a kid. His parents didn't say much, only saying something about a trip they took when he was a child, barely ten, to Utah, to some ranch. Rich people and their vacations," Max editorialized. "Anyway, apparently the boy was bitten by a wolf there."

"What?" I was completely taken aback.

"Yes, a tiny wolf bit him, there. It wasn't a pup but wasn't a big one, either. Brendan had wandered away from his parents for just a few minutes, and in that period of time, the animal attacked the child. Luckily, it left him alone after the bite, scampered away, though he did need hospitalization. Boy, this Brendan sure has had a strange life. But if you ask me, so have most rich people," he said, chuckling to himself.

"Anyway, the reason I mention this," Max, went on, "is that apparently young Brendan started having seizures after the incident. Nobody could figure out whether the two were connected. I mean, if the animal was infected with something or the other. But, Nancy, his mother, swears that his personality slowly started changing since that episode. He went on to do very well in school and seemed perfectly normal, but the mother always has those instincts, you know? She suspected something had changed with her son with that incident. His seizures were controlled with medication. And apparently, he had to be on them for life. I'm wondering whether he went off his meds?" Max wondered out aloud, really talking to himself.

"When he had his mental breakdown, you know, in his twenties?"

"So ... you're saying he's not a drug addict?" I poked holes in Max's theory.

"No, I'm just fielding different theories, here. Maybe he went off his meds and took drugs. Whatever it was, he's someone who'd experienced regular seizures after being bitten by a wolf. His mother claimed his personality slowly changed from that period of time and then, he'd had that breakdown. In NYU. I'm just saying this man is not stable. Imogen, don't be fooled by those blue eyes," Max said, looking at me impishly.

"Oh, come on, Max," I said, brushing aside his suggestive words. My mind was spinning. I'd heard of the legends and specifically, those of the Skinwalkers in Utah. Deep in the forests, magical creatures that could change shapes into other animals, and especially, wolves. Could it be possible that Brendan had been bitten by a Skinwalker? Could it be that that's why he was magical, and why I'd not sense any of the supernatural from either of his parents? It sounded outlandish, even to me. But nothing about Brendan's life had been normal. And my heart felt sorrow at the thought of the numerous seizures after the episode that he'd had to endure as a child. Maybe he'd indeed gone off his medication in his twenties. Maybe these medications had staved off the magic from surfacing in him. A magic that had been gifted to him by the Skinwalker, unfortunately. Something he had not sought out.

This was a theory, and a bizarre theory at that, but something about it resonated deeply within me. I tried to get the facts straight.

Brendan Connor was innocent. Brendan Connor was also supernatural. I knew he'd been bitten by a wolf. I knew he'd had seizures. And I knew that, what people were referring to as mental health issues, were probably manifestations of his supernatural self, something that he couldn't control. And so he escaped. He ran away and hid in the woods, quite literally.

I didn't know how I was going to do it, but I was determined to find a way to prove this man's innocence.

"And are you okay?" Max asked. I was completely lost in my own thoughts and had forgotten about Max standing right there.

"Oh, I'm fine. I'm just digesting all this information," I said.

"Well. He's out on bail now. But the charges won't be dropped. And there will be court proceedings and he will, most likely, be sent to jail, unless some miracle happens and he's able to prove his innocence by some means.

I nodded my head, understanding the gravity of the situation.

"Thanks, Max. I'm going head off, now. Go home now and ruminate on these things. Oh, and also deal with my dreadful husband, the divorce proceedings, updates on which I'm sure there's going to be pleasant reminders in my email inbox!"

"I'm sorry, Im," Max said, sympathetically.

I loved the way Max called me Im. It was a liberty only the people who were very familiar with me took. It meant he felt he was comfortable with me, and I liked that.

It meant he trusted me.

"Talk to you soon," I said, and we both parted ways. As I trundled up the avenues and streets and made my way home, with the chill air wafting over me and making me pull my coat closer to my body, I let my mind drift back to the mess in which my personal life was embroiled. My husband or soon-to-be ex-husband loomed to the fore of my mind's eye.

I pulled my cell phone out of my coat pocket and dialed my daughter. To my surprise, she picked up.

"Alexis, it's Mum, we need to talk." I was relieved I'd finally managed to catch her.

"Mum, this is not a good time," she said.

"You've been avoiding my phone calls the whole weekend. I'm your mother. I insist on speaking to you."

"Mum. I said it's not a good time. I'm trying to process everything that's happened over the dinner on Christmas Eve, okay? The horrible behavior that was displayed."

"Excuse me?" I said, stopping in my tracks for a long moment, taking in her cutting words.

"I'm not saying just by you, Mum, by everyone."

"Lexie, why are you being so kind towards ... " I started and then stopped. This was what I'd promised myself. That I was not going to draw my children into my ugly situation with Devlin. I was not going to turn them against their father, no matter who he might have turned out to be in the end.

"Yes, Mum?" Lexie persisted.

"Nothing," I said. "Forget it. But I'd like to see you. Will you please come home? I'd like to remind you that this is your home. Where you grew up. Not that apartment. Oh, come on, Lexie."

"Is it okay if I stay here for a few days? He's really shaken up," she said.

Why was my daughter showing so much empathy toward her father and so little toward me, her mother, the person that had been cheated on, the aggrieved party? I couldn't understand it, and it was breaking my heart. I knew if I'd stayed on the phone any longer, I would probably snap at her and say something cruel. I didn't understand it, but I didn't have the bandwidth to understand it at that moment. I needed to put the phone down, switch it off.

"Alexis, if you need anything, you know where to find me. You can come home any time, just wanted to let you know. If I don't see you before you head back to college, have a safe trip. I've got to go," I said, feeling my throat tighten with emotion, and I hung up.

The tears welled up in my eyes. Everything confused me at that moment, the situation with Devlin, a man I thought I'd known, my understanding of our marriage and the person I'd married, degrading with every step I was taking. And now, this dreadful situation with an innocent man who would most likely be convicted of a crime he didn't commit. Something had to give. As I was turning the corner onto my avenue, the phone rang again. It was Detective Max.

"Hey, Max, is everything okay?" I asked.

"I have some news," he said, sounding somber. "The forensic analysis of the bite marks on the bodies of the women. It was inconclusive; we couldn't prove they were a match to Brendan's."

Yes! I felt an incredible surge of relief wash over me. But it was quickly quelled.

"This doesn't mean anything, Imogen. It just means the test was inconclusive."

"I understand," I said.

After I hung up on Max, I felt a levity that I hadn't experienced in a while. You could argue that I was willing myself into believing someone to be innocent, but the truth was it's hard to explain the Faerie nature to someone who doesn't possess it. It's like a human instinct, but it is layered and textured and intense, and it is never wrong. It can be read wrong, but the instinct itself is pure. And with Brendan, I knew with certainty it wasn't an illusion. It was real.

Of course, those bite marks didn't belong to him. I made my way home and into my apartment, took off my coat, and turned up the heat. I was frozen from within. I checked my email on my laptop and found, to my dismay, that the lawyers were making it official. They were going to use the incident on Christmas Eve to demonstrate that I had a drinking problem. That I could not be trusted with inheriting a fortune. I couldn't believe what I was reading. Devlin was using mental incapacity as a reason to withhold money from me. It was ludicrous. Suddenly, a thought occurred to me: My situation was not unlike that of Brendan in some ways. His mental health was also being constantly questioned.

That must have worn him down; that must have been one of the reasons why he'd fled. Brendan's reasons were for things he couldn't spell out: they had to do with the supernatural realm. Magical things. My reason was that I had married poorly.

Devlin, my soon-to-be ex-husband, was turning out to be someone I couldn't recognize. A millionaire penny-pincher, looking to save as much money as he could. On reading that email, any illusion I'd had about Devlin shattered. After all those years of accrued memories, I realized that I must've been married to the illusion of someone. Or that he'd completely changed in the recent past. Whatever it was, I was done, trying to analyze it. It served no purpose anymore. Some things were beyond understanding.

Then, I had an epiphany. It occurred to me that I didn't have to prove to the world that I was of sane and solid mind. With Brendan, the thing that couldn't be explained was that he was supernatural. So, we had to find another way to prove his innocence! There was a murderer out there, and there would be other clues, ways to discern that somebody else was involved. I was determined not to let this train of thought go. I would pursue it to the end and try my very best to ensure that Brendan was released.

I looked at my cell phone. It was around half-past five. I opened the Internet browser on my laptop and started looking up Skinwalkers and Utah and lycanthropy. I spent a few hours reading up everything I could possibly find. People who'd been bitten by werewolves. People who'd been bitten by Skinwalkers. What had happened to them? Were there any records available? I read it all.

By the end of the evening, I was convinced. That while Brandon was born human, he'd had the supernatural infused into him with that life-changing trip to Utah. That the meds had kept his lycanthropy nature at bay. And for some reason, he must've got off of them in his early twenties, and then the true nature surfaced, leading to what people described as erratic behavior. I felt an incredible sense of pathos for this person. I knew what it felt to be misunderstood. We were both supernatural beings, but of course, here we were being misunderstood for different things. Implicated wrongly. I was going to get justice for Brendan even if I couldn't for myself.

New Year's Eve came and went in a hazy fog, with my mind oscillating between the drama with my family and Brendan. I thought about calling Bonnie over, but I knew she'd be busy with her kids, and I didn't feel like going over to her place, and having to deal with her entire family. I stayed by myself, feeling a bit self-piteous, and drank a bit too much red wine. What the hell? It was the holidays.

11

THE NEXT MONDAY, THE NEW YEAR greeting me with endless possibilities, and the weight of anticipation hanging in the air, I decided it was time to pay my office a visit. When I'd walked into the Manhattan Times office to meet my editor in the morning, the office was unusually abuzz with activity. There was heightened excitement in the air, and people whispering among themselves. And people were looking at me. It took me a few moments to realize that all eyes were turned toward me and fixated on me. I felt completely puzzled as I walked into my editor's office.

"Tony, what's going on?" I asked.

"You know, for someone in the journalism business, you're pretty slow at catching on to something," he said, looking at me wryly.

I balked at him. I didn't have a clue what he'd meant.

"I don't understand."

"You haven't picked up the papers at the newsstand this morning, I'm assuming?"

"No," I said, feeling a sense of discomfort.

"What happened?"

"Sit down, Imogen," Tony said and pulled up a copy of the Manhattan Times from his desk and tossed it toward me. And there, on the cover, was Brendan Connor's face, splashed across, and for all to see. The headlines read: "Billionaire Ted Connor's son found after 20 years. Suspected to be the Central Park serial killer."

My heart sank to the bottom of my feet.

"Oh, no," I whispered. I needed to sit down.

"Yes, indeed. Do you have anything to share with me?" Tony asked, suggestively.

I knew it was time to come clean, although my heart was racing with all the things I was reading.

"Yeah. Yes. So, I've been moonlighting with the NYPD. They wanted someone to provide them with a ... fresh perspective, so to speak. On cases they found difficult to solve."

Tony looked confused.

"I don't understand. You're a reporter. In what capacity do you serve them?"

I looked at my feet. This was not going to be easy. This was going to be very difficult. Tony was not only my editor, he was the reason I had my measly source of income at the newspaper. If my credibility came into question, my job could be in jeopardy.

"Okay, look Tony, I don't know how to explain this to you," I continued. "I believe in the supernatural powers. Psychic powers, you could call them," I said, flailing my arms about, trying hard not to make eye contact with him.

Tony looked at me utterly baffled.

"Well, let's just say you don't know what happens in my life outside of the work that I do for you, and I do good work for you. I have a friend in the NYPD, Detective Max Murphy, who believes I really am quite intuitive about people, psychic, even. Call it whatever. Anyway, so he asked me to come in. Believe it or not, the NYPD, once in a blue moon, asks psychics to assist with baffling cases and to see if they can be of any assistance. This happened to be the case into which I was called."

I finally made eye contact with Tony. "I know it sounds ludicrous to you, and all this is a lot to process, but I have bills to pay, and I know you don't know about this, but I have an impending divorce from a cheating husband. I need to make all the money that I can. So, I am properly defended in my divorce proceedings. I could lose everything, Tony," I said, looking at him imploringly.

After a really long silence, he finally spoke.

"Oh, my God, Imogen. I'm so sorry," he said,

I felt a profound sense of relief that he didn't laugh right at me.

"Why didn't you tell me any of this?" I stared at him.

"About the divorce, I mean?"

I nodded my head. I hadn't really thought about the reasons why.

"Why didn't you come to me if you were having money issues? Heck, marital issues. I'm your friend. We've known each other for so long," he said, empathetically.

"I guess I was embarrassed," I said. "And, by the way, I just found out he'd been cheating on me. It's just been recently that the whole thing caved in on itself. All of the missing pieces came together. He didn't tell me. I had to find out. And the most unpleasant of ways. It's just been a lot to process. But I do need to make more money."

"We could work out a way to maybe get you a full-time job here?" Tony said, looking at me inquisitively. With that comment, it became clear to me what Tony thought about my avocation.

"Thank you, Tony. That might very well be what I will have to do. But I'd like to see this assignment through with the NYPD."

There was an awkward pause as we stared at each other.

"You're working on this Central Park serial killer case? On the Brendan Connor case? This is incredible," he said, shaking his head.

To my surprise, he was pleased. Very pleased.

"You have first-hand information and insight into a case that all of Manhattan is talking about. The most sensational case of the year, probably the decade."

I could see where this was going.

"Tony, I have the greatest of respect for you, you know that. But I cannot and will not compromise my situation with the NYPD, for a story for the paper. I'm not in a position to discuss that case with you."

"Can you get us an interview?" he persisted, still trying his luck.

"No, Tony. I can't do that. He's a suspect. In a couple of gruesome murders. I have to follow protocol with the NYPD."

I stared at Tony expectantly, searching for that look of disappointment on his face, but it did not come. He looked at me for a long moment and then said, "Look at you, moonlighting as a sleuth," grinning from ear to ear. "I would have never guessed!" he said, sounding amused and with a smile on his face.

"And all this psychic stuff, you don't think I'm crazy?" I asked him.

"I honestly don't know what to think, but I feel for you, regarding the divorce, and I don't think your husband, that lying, cheating bastard, should get a single cent."

"Well, it's more like whether I'll get a single cent, Tony!" I said, facetiously.

"Well, then you do whatever you need to do to make the money you need to make. And remember, that full-time job offer is just around the corner, whenever you need it. "

"Thank you, Tony," I said, feeling a rush of relief and affection for my old friend. "Can I give you a hug?" I asked him.

"You know I don't do hugs, Imogen," he said.

I let my arms drop, but we both kept our small smiles.

"Damn shame," Tony said, as I was about to leave the office. "About the divorce."

"Tony," I said, "needless to say, please, can we keep this between us—that I'm working this case?"

"Look, I would, but it's a bit too late for that, Imogen," Tony said.

"What do you mean?" I asked, feeling perturbed.

"It's in some of the papers—the photos of you coming out of the precinct. People have got wind of the major players in this case, and they know that you're tied to it, now."

"Wait, is my name in the papers?" I asked, looking alarmed, and immediately thinking of my kids.

"Not yet, but your photo is there for all to see. It's not too obvious, don't be alarmed. You're in the background. Along with the detectives you'd mentioned. They're part of some feature in this, and also, in another paper about the case."

"Is that why the office has been staring at me this morning?"

"Yup. Don't worry, I won't say anything, but they're going to be bombarding you with questions, and you'd better come up with a solid answer."

"I'm not going to say anything to any of them!" I protested.

"Well, suit yourself," Tony said and then, turned back to his computer and started tending to his work. I left his office after submitting my latest article, I rushed back out of the building with all eyes still on me and picked up the phone and called Max.

"Hey Max. It's Imogen."

Oh, hi, Im. I can't talk right now. It's a little busy."

"Max, why didn't you tell me?"

"Yeah, I know you have seen the papers. We're being flooded with calls from reporters right now. The information leaked, we don't know how it happened, but everybody knows that Brendan Connor has been found and that he's a suspect, the prime suspect, in the Central Park murders. I was going to call you shortly and tell you myself. But I also figured you'd put two and two together before I did. I'm glad you're up to speed. I want to talk to you more, and I will, but this is not the moment. I've got to get back to work."

"Please keep me posted, okay?" I managed to squeeze in quickly before he hung up. My mind and heart were in a tizzy. I hailed a cab and made my way back home. I was weary from the excitement of the day. I needed some time to process everything and a strategy to help Brendan. And to help myself. Separate things. But were they, really? If I could somehow solve this case, for the NYPD, having the insight that I did into Brendan's situation, something none of them possessed., maybe this could mean a regular source of income for me. I could also get a full-time job with the Manhattan Times. That would mean more money, still. This would be a lot of work, and I hadn't worked long hours in a really long time, but something in me was fighting to come out, a voice that said, stand up for yourself and reclaim your life.

I didn't mind working hard. In fact, I looked forward to it. With my children gone and my husband deserting me, the thought of being completely engaged with something professional, provided me with a sense of great relief. I opened the fridge and was about to pour myself a glass of red wine, but then I remembered what the email from the divorce lawyers had said, earlier in the day. Alcohol abuse. I guffawed. I'm not addicted to this shit, I said to myself and shut the fridge.

I took a long shower and then sat on the couch in the living room and turned on the television. Channel after news channel, the only thing they were reporting on was Brendan Connor being found. Wolfman. Hiding in plain sight. Bite of the Devil. They went on and on. He was being vilified as the prime suspect in the Central Park case. Some channels equated him to the devil himself. The gossip was out of control. They were going to town on him. Spoiled, reckless, murderous millionaire Brendan Connor. Those were the headlines. They disgusted me, and I switched the television off.

I thought of my children. As I was about to retire for the night, the phone rang. I couldn't recognize the number and so, I picked it up, thinking it could be one of my kids. To my utter shock, it was Brendan Connor.

"Hi Imogen. It's Brendan. Connor."

"What? Brendan. Oh, hi. Hi," I said, sounding completely shocked. "What are you doing calling me?"

"Listen, I'm sorry to have done that. I know it's probably wrong."

"I'm working the case for the police, Brendan. I'm not supposed to be interacting with you outside of their purview."

"But, you're not really employed by the NYPD ... " he volunteered. I found this rude, and before I could respond, he said, "I'm sorry, I shouldn't have said that. I just wanted to give you a heads up. There is more news."

I braced for it.

"It's going to be in the papers tomorrow, that they've found my ... well, lair, as one of the reporters camped out of my house suggested. My belongings in the park. They found my campsite."

I listened quietly.

"Apparently, my lawyer tells me they were located very close to where both the murders had happened. I know this—I clarified this. I did mention to the detectives that I'd heard both the women being attacked in some capacity or the other and had gravitated toward the sound. But my lawyer told me to brace for it being reported in the papers as something else. Something sinister. That I was right where the murders had happened. You know, they'll spin-doctor it. It'll reek of guilt."

I didn't know what to say. I couldn't believe I was on the phone with Brendan.

"I'm feeling terrible, Imogen. And I think I'm going to go to prison. I think I'm going to spend the rest of my life there," he said.

I could hear the tears in his voice. I really was at a loss for words. The truth was it did look really, really bad.

"Look, we'll find a way. You said you saw the face of the murderer? Maybe, with the permission of your lawyer and the NYPD, we can meet again, and you can describe this person in greater detail to me. Have you talked about him to the cops? Maybe you can get a sketch artist from the NYPD to draw the person for you?"

"We're doing that. My lawyer is pursuing every legal option," he said, sounding distant.

I really felt for him. Then he said, "You said you believed me."

It suddenly occurred to me: how did he get my number?

"How did you get my number?" I asked.

It's not difficult these days, Imogen."

"Uh huh," I responded.

I finally said: "Yes Brendan, I do believe you're innocent."

It is at that moment that I'd realized he hadn't a clue of my Faerie background. He didn't possess the intuitive powers I did. I'd known he wasn't a faerie, I could clearly sense that, but I hadn't been sure of what sort of supernatural being he was. Although I was leaning towards lycanthropy, knowing his past, I knew I couldn't reveal my identity to him. There was simply no way I was going to do that. It would jeopardize everything, things beyond my comprehension, even.

"So, as you know, I work as a psychic for the NYPD," I continued. I'd given this explanation enough times that I knew how to say it without giving myself away. "I just have a strong instinct about people."

"So, it's your instinct that's convinced you of my innocence?" Brendan responded. He sounded disappointed. The voice within me was screaming to tell him the truth. One supernatural being to another. I knew this was one person who would understand. But I couldn't do it.

"Yes, it's an instinct, Brendan, that is all. But I'd like to point out that, for whatever reason, the NYPD has entrusted me to be part of this case, and every opinion matters. And my opinion is that you're innocent. Which means it probably isn't a good idea for me to be talking to you on the phone outside of regularized channels." I was at my wit's end and didn't have anything useful left to say.

"I understand," he said, with his voice almost a whisper.

"Listen, you haven't seen your parents in a really long time. You've been in a faraway place in your mind, for so long. Everything probably feels really confusing to you now. And yes, you face the threat of it all being taken away again. It's okay to feel upset and confused, Brendan. In fact, I'd be surprised if you weren't feeling those things. But, I suggest you use this time to ... and forgive me for taking the liberty ... to bond with your parents who've missed you terribly. Enjoy good food. Drink a glass of wine. Listen to good music. Watch the tele ... actually, don't watch the television. It might be upsetting," I added, feeling foolish for suggesting it.

He just said, "Okay."

There was so much I wanted to ask and there was so much I wanted to share. I wasn't permitted to do either. It tormented me.

"So, I'd better go," he said.

'Before you hang up," I quickly asked, "Where were you all these years?" My curiosity got the better of me.

"I thought I wasn't supposed to interact about these things outside of the regularized channels?"

"You're right, I'm sorry I asked."

"I was in the park," he said.

"What?"

"I was in Central Park."

"For twenty years?"

"Yes."

I was about to ask him how he had not been discovered, but realized I'd already reached the end of my tether with respect to behaving irresponsibly. This job meant a lot to me. I was tired and had processed about as much information as I could for the day.

"You're right, Brendan. It's not right for us to be talking outside of the proper channels. Trust your lawyer and trust that the law will set you free if you're innocent. Which I believe you are."

"But the law has nothing to do with ... "

"Nothing to do with ... ?" I asked, trying to get him to finish his sentence.

"Nothing, forget what I said," Brendan said. And then he hung up.

My heart ached for this man. A victim of circumstance. Trapped by something he hadn't asked for. And living a destitute life in the middle of Central Park for all these years, away from his parents, who'd thought he was dead. And then, it occurred to me. Why he'd probably chosen Central Park. It was right next to where his parents lived. I was utterly moved by his situation. Brendan had been through enough pain and suffering. And I was going to do everything I could in my capacity to ensure that he was exonerated.

12

·

THE NEXT DAY, I WOKE UP TO A FEELING that was different. Like the whole world had changed somehow, by just a little. I couldn't quite put my finger on it, but it was like an emotional door had been opened up inside me, so deep inside that I couldn't quite comprehend its gravity. The imperceptible change was ever so slight, except it was in everything that I was seeing and doing. I felt a purpose in my life. I felt clear-headed after a long time.

I got up, brushed my teeth, put on a pot of coffee, and turned on the television. Then reality hit me. The headlines. The thing that was making the news, it was horrible. Brendan Connor. *Wolfman.* The media had strung together bits of superfluous information – about the fact that he'd purportedly bit people near the park, that he had been found unkempt and with hair overgrown. The animal montage seemed a befitting response to generate more paper sales.

Serial killer. Rich, spoiled brat, turned murderer. Narcissistic deviant. The headlines went on, each worse than the next, and I had to turn the television off, again. This was not going to go away, I quietly realized. Something drastic had to be done.

My heart was aflutter. My mind was racing, I couldn't believe how far the truth was from what was actually reality. Brendan was nothing like what these people were making him out to be. He was innocent, first and foremost. And, he was trapped. In possession of a supernatural gift he hadn't asked for and with a mind that was, as a result, playing tricks on him. He's paid the price and then some. He'd suffered painful seizures in his childhood and youth. He'd tried his best to surpass this aspect of his life, working hard and doing well in school and then, in college. He'd had a steady girlfriend. He'd made his parents proud. And then ... everything unraveled. Just because life can sometimes, just like that, for no rhyme or reason.

Our lives can be split asunder in a second. And then, we're forced to grapple with the wreckage that is left behind. The sound of his voice echoed in my head. The pain he felt. He'd met his parents after twenty long years, and he was going to be ripped apart from them again. People made irrational, linear connections between money and immorality, and that was what the media was doing here. Never mind that Brendan had been far removed from the world of privilege for decades. He'd been lost inside his mind and struggling inside Central Park, battling the demons that were unknown to the world outside. But that wasn't what the media was going to report.

No. All they saw was a monster. Rich kid, serial killer, a deviant. Someone who had been given every privilege and had thrown it all away.

I tried to put things in perspective. I knew he was not mentally ill, but even if he'd had mental challenges, what would that have had to do with his bank balance and his mental health. His psychiatric history had been well recorded. Why wasn't any attention being given to that? Why weren't people talking about his purported mental illness?

I was reminded of that famous quote from Shakespeare's *Julius Caesar*. When Mark Anthony said, "The evil that men do lives after them; the good is oft interred with their bones."

Except this man was not dead, he was alive and fighting for his life. I needed to get out of the apartment. I put on my winter coat and my boots, took my phone and keys, and left the suffocating space. I wasn't sure where I was headed, but I wanted some fresh air. I walked past the expensive apartment buildings where incredibly wealthy folks lived their comfortable lives and were speculated on by the rest of struggling humanity. I walked past upmarket stores and cafes. And then, I saw the newsstand, packed with newspapers and magazines with headlines that said horrible things about Brendan Connor. The anger in me fomented. I felt the unfairness of it all viscerally, deep within me, with every passing moment. I was in a foul mood.

I thought of my daughter and decided to act against what I'd known, from experience, to be my better judgment. I knew they were going to be consequences to calling my daughter in an agitated state, but I had to know. I was sick of being in the dark about people's motivations for their behaviors. This was a child I'd had given birth to and loved from the core of my being.

Lexie picked up.

"So, my darling girl ... do you plan on coming home? Do you plan on going back to school?" I couldn't help it. I knew when I saw someone drifting away from the path they were meant to be on, and this was my daughter.

"Hi, Mum. Firstly, I'm not avoiding you. I've just been worried about Dad and have wanted to keep an eye on him. After all, Justin was with you."

"Yes, he was. He's gone now, he's been gone for a few days. Lexie, look, I have to be honest with you. I'm befuddled. I'm not trying to accuse you of anything or play one parent against the other, but I do want to talk with you and I want to talk with you today in person. Now. I'm on Fifth and Sixty-Third street. I can walk across to Madison Avenue. Let's meet at that cafe around the corner from your dad's apartment building? I can be there in fifteen minutes. I really want to see you. I need to."

"Mum, I can't meet right now," Lexie replied immediately.

"What are you doing that's so important? Lexie, since you clearly don't have plans to be going back to school anytime soon ... "

"It's Thursday. I decided to stay here for another week; community college will not crumble into dust. I can catch up. It's not an issue."

"If you say so. But I'd like to meet,' I said, trying hard to speak with restraint.

There was a long pause at the end of the line.

"I really don't want to fight, Mum."

I took a deep breath and then slowly exhaled it out into the crisp air.

"I don't want to fight my daughter, either. I love you. I just want to talk."

"Okay," she finally said.

In about fifteen minutes, I was sitting at the café, waiting impatiently for my daughter. I'd found a seat by the window and looked out at the pedestrians walking up and down the street purposefully. Everybody always looks so purposeful in Manhattan. I wondered if all of these people had thoughts like mine, of uncertainty, of confusion. Were they all as sure-footed as they looked?

"Hi, Mum," Lexie's voice interrupted my reverie. My heart immediately melted upon seeing my beautiful daughter, my second born.

"Hello, darling." I got up and gave my daughter a deep hug.

She then sat in the chair across from me, and we both looked at each other for a silent moment. I smiled.

160

"So, how's it going?" I asked, speaking with a mild demeanor, not wanting to jump on her at the very beginning.

"Oh, it's okay. You know."

"No, I don't know. Tell me, dear," I said, still smiling.

"Mum, stop, okay? You said you're not going to pick on me."

"I'm not picking on you, darling! But we're allowed to have a conversation."

"Okay," she said, looking uncomfortable.

"Look, it's been weighing on me the last few days," I said, unsure of how to segue to everything I'd wanted to talk about with my daughter. "I know I haven't reached out the last day or two, but that's because things at work were extremely pressing."

"Oh, you mean with your part-time journalism job?" Alexis said, carelessly.

"There. That's it. That's what I'm talking about. That's what I want to talk about today. Your need to put me down constantly. A job is a job, Lexie. You will realize the dignity involved in having and maintaining a job when you are out in the real world making your own way. And no, I'm not talking about my *part-time* journalism job, as you put it, which I happen to love, by the way. I've taken on some consulting work. It's regarding something I don't wish to talk about it. Can't talk about it. I'm here to talk about *you*, my daughter. I've been trying to understand something ... "

Alexis looked at me expectantly.

"If there is a reason why you're angry with me, why you feel the need to be passive-aggressive towards me, which you clearly are, I'd like to know what is."

"Mum! I'm not angry with you," Lexie said, rolling her eyes.

"You constantly take digs at me," I said, flatly. "And that's not just the past few days, but the past maybe year or two. You constantly belittle me. I was willing to put up with it, thinking of it as teenage angst or youthful rebellion or whatever you want to call it. But that night, that Christmas Eve dinner ... "

Alexis immediately stiffened.

"I don't want to talk about that evening."

"Well, we're going to talk about some aspects of it," I said flatly.

She stared at me silently.

"Look, it's very apparent to me that you feel a great deal of empathy for your father in this situation," I worded myself very carefully. "I guess I'm trying to understand why."

"He's not a monster, Mum."

"I never said he was. I wouldn't have married a monster."

"You poured a bottle of wine onto his head!" Alexis raised her voice. I held my ground, though I was breaking inside.

"I'm sorry, do you have selective memory?" I asked my daughter. "Do you not recall what he said just before that? What he called me. Are you not aware by now what has happened? The proof there in that awful evening's proceedings? That he cheated on me, that he had an affair for a year with another woman while we were married."

"People make mistakes," Alexis said. That was her first response.

"Goddamn it, Lexie," I shouted. People in the cafe went silent and heads turned to look at us.

"There you go again," she said.

I really wanted to throw my cup of coffee at her face. She was trying to make me out to be someone I was not. Paint a narrative simply because it suited her at that moment to think of me that way. I tried to understand why she was behaving that way, and then, suddenly, it hit me.

"You're trying to make me out to be the villain," I said, staring at her, searching her eyes for any clue that I was getting through to my daughter.

"I'm really not, Mum. okay?"

"You're trying to make me out to be lesser than I am, and I will not allow you, my daughter, to do that to me. In fact, I will not allow *anybody* to do that to me. Not my husband, not my children, not this world. I've had to overcome enormous hardships to come to this country and start from scratch. I never had access to the privileges you take for granted. And perhaps that has been the problem. And for that, I own up to my mistakes. I was too lenient with you. I see that now. But now, you've got a glimpse of life with your father. And you see possibly that, oh I don't know, my own life is taking a downturn in your eyes ... "

"Mum, that's not it," Lexie tried to interrupt, but I'd had enough.

"Let me finish!" I harshly interjected. "I think you want to be with the person that you see is winning."

She looked at me with searing eyes.

"Say something!" I nearly screamed. "Is this true, Lexie? Is this why you're behaving the way you are, siding with the person who clearly, obviously did wrong in this situation? Because you think you'll have a more comfortable life, leaning toward your father?"

And for the first time, I saw on my beautiful daughter's face, a look of recognition I'd never seen before. She looked ashamed. My normally loud and vociferous daughter stayed completely silent, staring at her feet. A long and painful moment passed in silence.

"Since you are not offering any alternative explanations, and judging by the expression on your face, I'm to assume this is the case. Well, let me tell you something, my dear daughter. You might think you're siding with what is better, but what you're actually siding with is taking the easy way out in life. Aligning yourself with the person who seems stronger at that moment than the other and not with what's right versus wrong. It's not the way I would've wanted to have raised my children. I am worried for you, I think you're getting your priorities all mixed up and despite the hurt you've caused me, are causing me, I'm concerned about you."

164

"Don't be, Mum," came the steely reply. I saw a look I hadn't seen on my precious daughter's face before.

"I'm doing fine," she reiterated.

"I don't think you are, not really. You might appear fine on the surface, but Lexie, somewhere deep within, you're morphing into what people refer to as a social climber." The moment the words left my mouth, I knew they were a mistake. I wanted the earth to open up and swallow me whole.

"How dare you?" she spat at me. Eyes in the room turn toward us.

"I'm not the one who married above me. And like you said, I'm born into wealth. Why would I want to 'social climb' when I have all the money in the world?"

Tears streamed freely down my face at this point.

"You do not have money! Your father has money, and like he is demonstrating right now, toward his own wife, he can take it away any time he wants. Is that how you want to live, Lexie? Someone who depends on another's money and whimsy and temperament, in your life? And let me tell you, a man who is willing to take away money from a woman he has been unfaithful toward, his wife of twenty years whom he has wronged, will not think twice about doing that to another person. Even his own daughter."

"Aren't you ashamed of yourself?" Alexis said to me. I stared at my daughter blankly, unable to process what I was witnessing. The girl she had become. "You're putting down your own husband."

"Yes. My soon to be ex-husband. I'm just saying for your own good, don't depend on anybody else, much less people who are fickle."

"If Dad were fickle, he wouldn't have been able to work hard and make the kind of money he has."

"He worked hard and made the kind of money he did because he had strong family support. A partner stood by side. Took care of his family and children. Provided him with a sense of psychological security. Encouragement, love, and support. Which he frankly, didn't get from his own family growing up. This probably cannot be monetized in your eyes, but it is real, Lexie. These things are real. I'm scared for you that you don't see that. Justin does."

"Fine, you've got your precious son. What do you need me for?"

"It's not a competition. You sound like a child, Lexie. Grow up. Realize that morals and values do count in the long race, and life is a long race. You will not win it by siding with what's convenient. And remember, someday you will have to make money of your own. Or you will face a situation where you have to stand on your own, on the back of your own morals. You will find yourself frightfully alone on that day if this is the direction in which you're headed."

"And what direction is that, Mum? Leading an empty life like you are?" Tears started welling up in my daughter's eyes as she got up to leave.

"Lexie! Sit down, I'm not done talking."

"I'm done listening," she said. "People cheat in marriages, mum. You grow up. I don't know what planet you're from, but it happens all the time. I'm sorry you're hurting, Mum. But the things you're calling me, they're not true. I stay with Dad because he values me."

"I value you," I argued in vain.

"No, you don't. You prefer Justin. Dad dotes on me. It's okay. It's all karma." She sounded like an unevolved brat.

"If I'm hard on you or have been hard on you in the past, it's because I want you to be the best version of yourself. That's what true love is."

"Well, you've got a community college-going daughter who's happy sponging off her rich father."

I wanted to say something but I really didn't have any fight left in me, anymore. I felt defeated and brokenhearted. The day had begun so well and now, it was taking a downturn. I suddenly felt old. I had a daughter who was grown up enough to realize the gray areas in life and was creating a world for herself where morals were ambiguous and movements were calculated. This was not the life I'd wanted for my child.

After Lexie left the café, I sat there silently staring at my coffee. It had gone cold. A smattering of rain had started outside. I paid the bill wearily and left the restaurant. It was only drizzling, so I decided to brave walking back home. Where had I gone so wrong with my child? Had I really been that lenient with her when she was growing up?

My thoughts were racing, of my family, my disintegrating family, and I was far removed from the case at that moment, so when the phone rang, I was shaken back into reality. It was Detective Max Murphy.

"Hey, Max. What's going on?"

"Hey, Im. Are you okay? You sound kind of off. Are you alright?"

"Yes, I'm fine, thank you. Well, as good as can be in these circumstances."

"Well, if you're not in a good mood, brace yourself, because you're going to be ecstatic when you hear what I have to say. "

"What happened," I asked, immediately on alert.

"I have some news. I can't classify it as either good or bad, but I know you're gonna love it."

"Max! Go ahead, hit me with it!" I said impatiently.

"Your pal, Brendan. He's off the hook.'

I stopped dead in my tracks. The noise and sounds of the world around me completely vanished in the background.

"What do you mean?" I asked, slowly, unable to process the information.

"Well, that's coming to the bad news. There's been another horrific murder last night in Central Park. The body was discovered this morning by a jogger. Similar M.O. Young woman. Bludgeoning. Bite marks. Torn body. It wasn't Brendan obviously, because he was home with his family and being watched by detectives."

"You had detectives on him?" I focused on a detail. The street was spinning.

"Come on, Im. We're not amateurs here."

I felt a sense of relief that I couldn't quite describe in words; it was overwhelming. I was elated for Brendan. And yet, there had been another tragic and senseless murder.

"Any clues at the site?" I asked, reminding myself of my professional purpose in all of this. I was here to help the NYPD, not be Brendan's personal cheerleader. He was off the hook! He was going to be fine now.

"The police have cordoned off the area and are searching the woods, but this case is completely baffling. The perpetrator. Apart from the bite marks, he leaves no hair or blood or saliva or semen. No bodily fluids. You name it, there's nothing on the site. No fingerprints, even. Nada. Not even in the bite marks. It's perplexing."

"Alright," I said to Max, 'thanks for letting me know of the update." My mind was already racing forwards to Brendan. "Let me know how I can help, Max. I'm here for that, you know that."

"Okay, sure. They're probably going to be rounding up some usual suspects in the area. Petty criminals and the like. Talk to them, interrogate them, see if we can come up with any leads. And we're going to talk to Brendan further. We need to find out more ... about what he knows regarding the person he saw. Right now, he's our strongest lead. He's the only one who's witnessed the man who committed these murders. We need detailed physical descriptions, anything really, that we can cling on to."

"I'm sure he will cooperate," I said. "Do you want me to talk to him?" I asked, a bit too eagerly.

"No, Im. We'll do that, of course. But you were right. That bloody Faerie instinct of yours. It was completely dead-on. Brendan was innocent. The poor guy was vilified by the press. At least now maybe they'll back off."

"Yeah, they don't think twice about ripping into people without confirming the facts first. "

"Well, that's the way the news works, Im, you of all people know this. But, not to worry, in twenty-four hours, they'll be on to something else. Good job, though. I'm certainly going to be using you. Your services. Henceforth."

"I'm here to help," I said.

"Oh, and there's the matter of payment. I've talked to management. I will be in touch with you on that."

"Oh, don't worry about it."

"Come on, Imogen, we know that's what you're doing this for," Max added. "No need to be coy about it."

The truth was, the money had receded into the background, even though that had been my original reason for taking on this job. All I could think about was Brendan, and meeting a kindred spirit whom I now had helped prove was innocent. My heart was racing with extremes of emotions in one day.

It's hard enough to handle being a middle-aged woman, staking out new careers, and dealing with divorces at the same time. Reinventing ourselves. But I was acting like a teenager. Perhaps it was this heady mix of emotions in my head that made me behave the way I did over the next few minutes because what I did, ended up changing a lot of things. Permanently. I searched for Brendan's number, which I'd saved on my phone, judiciously. And before I'd had time to dissuade myself from doing it, I'd dialed his number. In retrospect, I can't say why I did it with such certainty, but it'd felt as natural as the clear light of day.

The familiar, throaty voice answered.

"Hi, Brendan. It's Imogen. Imogen McLelland."

"Yes, I know. I've got your number, remember?" he said. I could hear the smile in his voice. He sounded cheerful.

"Well, I just wanted to say ... oh, I don't know what you're supposed to say in these circumstances. But, congratulations, I guess?" I offered nervously.

"Thank you," he replied. "You were the only one who believed that I was innocent the whole time. Thank you for helping me get my name cleared."

"Oh, I didn't do anything. Not really. It was a tragic twist of events that has led to this situation. But whatever it is, you were innocent and you were being persecuted and that needed to stop. Now, you can get on with the rest of your life. I mean, you know, pick up the pieces. No, sorry, what I meant was ... "

"Imogen," he said, interrupting my disastrous trail of words.

"No, I get it," I said, nervously laughing. "You have to go. You probably have a busy evening ahead of you. Celebrating, and all that," I said. I sounded like an idiot.

Brendan had been chained within his mind for years, and now, he was back with his family. On the cusp of great news. He probably, obviously, wanted to celebrate.

Don't let your mind race, Imogen, I said to myself. But Brendan completely surprised me.

"Imogen, would you like to have dinner with me tonight?" he asked, plainly and simply.

Now, I want to say, I took a moment longer than I did to respond. I want to say that I was calm and composed, and then pretended to be completely surprised. But the truth was I wasn't any of those things, because all I'd wanted was to enable a situation like this to play out in my wildest fantasies. Except, this wasn't a fantasy. It was actually happening. It was real.

I simply said *yes.*

We met at Scardino's at half-past seven for dinner. Brendan had reserved a private room for our meal because he didn't want the prying eyes. He was still in the thick of a storm of conjecture and malicious news. His name was rooted in the subconscious of the public, and it was going to be sometime before people stopped looking at him as a strange and discomfiting figure. He was going to have to work for his privacy. He had a long road ahead, but he was on the right path. He'd made a start to get his name back, and here he was sitting across the table from me. Ridiculously handsome. Clean-shaven and smelling of cologne. And the waiters in this Michelin star restaurant, if they'd known of his infamy, were much too polite to show it.

It was awkward in the beginning. There should have been no reason for the two of us to be having dinner together, now that the case, at least for Brendan's innocence, had been concluded. But the staring hadn't stopped. He kept staring at me. I felt like I was back in the interview room, where we'd first met, and the uneasiness over the moral grayness of what I was doing right then, sunk in. Maybe it was the years spent away from civilization that'd made him forget his manners, but Brendan kept looking at me and it made my cheeks flush. Which he also noticed.

"You're flushed," he said, casually.

"It must be the red wine," I said.

We'd ordered generous amounts of ridiculously expensive Merlot, and the music was playing softly in the background. It was just the two of us. I could ask him anything that I wanted, now that his name was cleared and my safety assured. I wanted to get straight to the heart of the matter. I wanted to ask him about his supernatural powers. And that was the *one* thing I couldn't do. I couldn't risk it, not yet. I didn't know anything about him.

What had he been up to the last two decades? And after what I'd been through with my husband, I wasn't ready to trust another man with my deepest secrets, not without a fight. Yet, I'd felt I had stumbled into a dream that evening. I was wearing a short black dress and black stilettos. I did look a bit too dressed up for an evening that hadn't been classified as a date. I'd spent a little too much time getting ready, and so I'd toned down the makeup, and let my raven hair fall naturally on my shoulders. To an objective observer, we might have looked like brother and sister, with striking black hair and blue eyes. But they would have soon guessed otherwise, looking at the way in which we were looking at each other.

"Tell me about yourself," Brendan broke the ice, thankfully.

"Well, I grew up in Scotland. That's where I'm from. In a small village actually, called Killin. I came here over twenty years ago."

"Why did you leave?"

"Oh, there was some unhappiness there. Besides, I was young and wanted to see the world, and escape from the village life, really. But where I'm from, it's a beautiful place. Idyllic. Perthshire. Or Sterling, as it's now called."

"Fascinating," Brendan said.

"Oh, not really, I was just a small-town girl who had bigger dreams."

"I guess village life is not for everyone."

Something about the way he spoke. I could see that he wanted to speak honestly. I was looking for a way to trust him, so I opened up a little.

"Actually, I'm not being honest with you. Truth be told, I loved my life in Killin. I loved the village life. And I'd known since childhood, exactly what I'd wanted to become, which was a doctor, a surgeon. I got into medical school in a city close to Killin. Dundee. This was when I was eighteen—you go to med school in undergrad back in Scotland," I volunteered.

He listened patiently. And I wasn't sure where I was going with this, because at some point I'd have to start covering up the bad parts. And the Faerie ways. But I continued, anyway.

"But just when I was about to head off to medical school in Dundee, my childhood sweetheart, Michael, who was to accompany me, died. Drowned. In a local river."

"Oh, my God, Imogen," Brendan said, looking shocked. "I'm so sorry."

"Yes, well, that was a long time ago, but it shattered me."

The narrative seemed to provide enough justification for leaving Scotland, so I said simply, "And so I left."

"Do you miss home?" he asked.

I tried to stop my voice from quivering: "More than I can possibly explain or articulate."

"Do you see your parents often?"

Now, this was getting uncomfortable. "No, But, let's talk about you a little," I said, trying to smile. It came across as awkward.

"Sure, I suppose that's fair," he said. "You've been honest with me. But wait, before I tell you about myself, are you married?" he asked. I was taken aback by the question. My cheeks flushed again. It hadn't occurred to me that he'd seen my wedding band, which was still on my ring finger. I'd completely forgotten to remove it.

"Oh, my God. You think I'm a married woman. Well, I am. Wait, I'm getting divorced."

"I'm sorry to hear that," he said, trying to keep up with my jabbering.

It'd all come out in a bit of a jumble.

"I recently found out that my husband of two decades, father of my two children, whom I'd met as soon as I'd come from Scotland and thought of as the love of the second chapter of my life, has been sleeping with another woman. Since last year. He'd been cheating on me."

I don't know why I was sharing so much. I hadn't been out with a man in a really long time, and I was rusty. But it was also Brendan's disarming nature that made me instinctually open up.

"Very sorry to hear that," Brandon said, looking genuinely contrite.

"Yes, it's been a rough couple of weeks. The children, Justin and Lexie, are torn up about it, and even though I swore to keep them out of it, it looks like they're embroiled in the politics of it all, inevitably. And the fact that his beautiful, blonde doctor girlfriend is almost half his age, well, that's just the cherry on the parfait, isn't it?" I said, smiling and taking a large sip of the red wine.

"Why do men do this?" Brendan opined, commiserating with me.

"I don't know why you folks do it, but apparently it happens all the time, as my daughter recently helpfully pointed out, and even though everyone thinks it won't happen to them, it happened to me. It feels surreal, frankly. I think I'm still too close to the events as all of this just came to the fore, recently. But I haven't wrapped my brain around it yet." I wanted to change the subject.

"Besides, I got caught up with a rather interesting case with the NYPD involving a mysterious man, who has since been exonerated, and it has kept me busy," I said, smiling at Brendan. He realized it was time to offer some information.

"Oh, there's nothing much to it, really. I had some sort of a nervous breakdown when I was in my junior year in college. Partied a bit too much. I guess my parents didn't like it."

He wasn't looking at me, he looked distracted and was glancing around the room as he spoke.

"And so I was committed to a mental health facility, and I ran away from there! Yup!" he said in a self-deprecatory manner and took a large swig from his wine glass.

None of it made sense, I knew he was lying. He knew that I knew he was lying, but he was sticking with that narrative. I was trying to find the perfect segue to get him to open up, but really, there was no easy segue to *Tell me about your lycanthropy.* There was no real avenue. I wanted to poke holes in his flimsy, rather ridiculous-sounding story, but I didn't want to upset him or ruin the mood of the evening. I couldn't get over how handsome he looked, nor could I ignore the visceral attraction between us.

I wish I could say it was just physical, but there was something far deeper to it. It was metaphysical. We were drawn to each other, and I knew why I was drawn to him. His goodness. His pain. His mystical powers. All of it resonated with me. But his lycanthropy didn't permit him to see that I was a supernatural being as well. I wanted to tell him. I wanted to get him to open up.

So, I changed the subject instead, talking about my kids and about how Lexie was proving to be a real handful. How I was afraid she was turning out to be just like her father. Conceited and calculating. I told him about my upsetting afternoon meeting with my daughter. About how proud I was of my son and him studying to be a doctor.

"Does it bother you?" Brendan suddenly asked.

"What?" I asked, momentarily confused.

"To see your son preparing to go to medical school when you couldn't, yourself?"

Normally, in the past, when someone had asked me that question, and it had happened on occasion, it would bother me deep within, but when Brendan asked me, it didn't offend me at all. In fact, it comforted me. And for the first time in my life, I answer truthfully:

"I'm immensely proud of my son. I'm so glad he's going into such a noble profession and living out his dreams. Yes, it hurts that I couldn't get to do that for myself. But the two are not really connected. It is bittersweet, I guess you could say."

"Thanks for being honest," Brendan said, smiling at me. "You know," he added, "it's probably not my place to say this, but maybe Lexie senses how proud you are of Justin and feels insecure. Maybe that's part of why she's lashing out."

"I love both my kids equally," I said.

"I don't doubt that you do. But I can tell you, the need to impress our parents never goes away. And sometimes, we'd rather put on a brave face or hide from them than let them see how much their opinion matters to us," he said, looking away. I understood what he'd meant.

After a fabulous dinner, Brendan asked if he could walk me back to my apartment. I was fine with it. In fact, I felt safe knowing that there was a predator on the loose, not to be walking home alone, and so close to the park. The restaurant was just around the block from my own apartment building.

"Your husband, soon to be ex-husband, must be pretty successful, for you to be staying in this place," he said bluntly when we reached my building. I pardoned his candor. He'd been away for a long time. I would cut him some slack.

"Well, it won't be for much longer, if he has his way. He's going to take everything from me. He's citing alcohol abuse as one of the reasons why he thinks I shouldn't be left in charge of large sums of money."

"What a prick!" Brendan swore. "You were perfectly fine at dinner."

"I don't have a problem, Brendan. He just … doesn't want to let go of the money he made. I don't know, he doesn't seem to have much empathy for me, even though he's the one who cheated on me. Go figure. It's complicated. And I don't have the energy to try to figure it out."

"You should fight it," Brandon said.

"I am, but lawyers are expensive. That's why I took on the gig with the NYPD, and now, I'm probably going to go work full-time at the *Manhattan Times*. I should be fine taking care of myself, and Devlin will never do anything to jeopardize the children's future. I think. So, we're good."

"You don't think it's going to be tough?" Brendan asked. "Giving all this up?"

"I've given up far more to come to this country. It's just money at the end of the day. It doesn't hurt, but it's not going to save our souls. Besides, it's time."

"Time for what?" he prodded.

"Time to meet some of that potential I possessed when I was a child. Something about the last few weeks, it's lit a spark in me. Made me realize I'm a lot more resilient than I'd imagined I was."

"Good for you, Imogen," he said, sounding impressed. "But, really, you should fight for what is yours on principle. While he was off making his millions, you raised a family, took care of his home."

"I know," I said. "I'm not going to let him get away with it without a fight. Hurting my reputation, that is. He can have his money."

"Don't do that, don't undervalue yourself."

"It's funny you should say that," I said to Brendan. "I was just telling my daughter this afternoon, that you might not be able to monetize the love and support a wife provides to a spouse. But it does have a real value, you know," I said ruefully.

"Well, I'm saying the opposite. I'm saying you *can* monetize that value and you should. It's what's due to you! Because he should realize what he did was wrong. And that it comes at a cost. Sorry, sorry, I'm preaching," Brendan said.

"Yes, you are," I agreed, and we both laughed. "You know, for someone who has so many clear and strong views on so many things, I've yet to piece together the puzzle that is Brendan Connor."

"I have a suspicious feeling you will," he said. Maybe it was the way he smiled at me, maybe it was the way the moonlight struck his black hair and made it shimmer. Maybe it was the wine. I don't know, but I blurted out, "Would you like to come up for a cup of coffee?"

Brendan went wide-eyed and then, he smiled and said, "No, not tonight, Imogen, but thank you for a wonderful evening."

I felt a profound rush of embarrassment and my heart sank to my feet. My cheeks flushed, again, but thankfully, Brendan was too much of a gentleman to point it out.

"I really should get going. Thank you for a great evening," he said and then turned toward the street and hailed a cab. I was cursing myself for being so forward with him. *What was I thinking? It was our first ... well, it wasn't even a date, it was just dinner. And straight away, I invite him up to my apartment. Jesus.*

As the cab sped away, I turned around and entered my building. Brendan had made me feel something I'd never felt with Devlin. Nor with Michael, even. What that was, is hard to describe. Maybe it was a sense of meeting an equal. A kindred spirit. Or maybe it was being attracted to a man whose ego wasn't constantly getting in the way. Brendan seemed devoid of all of that. Yet there was so much to him that I didn't know. And meanwhile, I had to live in reality amidst the shambles of my marriage. And the growing bills. As I made my way up the elevator and into my apartment, I smiled to myself. *You dumbass. You just invited Brendan Connor up to your apartment. For coffee. Right.*

And on the day he was acquitted of being a serial killer. I thought of that and burst out laughing. And once I started laughing, I couldn't stop. A sense of levity, the kind I'd experienced rarely, had returned into my being. It really was the first time that I'd allowed myself a good laugh in a very, very long time and I savored every moment of it.

13

WHEN I WOKE UP THE NEXT MORNING, I realized I had nothing to do. I'd met certain deadlines with the *Manhattan Times*, my children weren't home—one in school and the other with her father, and Brendan was off the hook. I had absolutely nothing to do. It felt glorious. I lay in bed staring at the ceiling as the early morning light filtered in through the windows. I thought of the previous evening with Brendan, and the incredible attraction I'd felt to this man who was at the center of the storm.

Somehow, my connection seemed separate from all of the noise surrounding the case. When we were at the restaurant, it felt like we were in our own private universe. On our own island, an island of hope. I tried to check myself. *Stop getting ahead of yourself*, I muttered out loud. *You still don't know much about this man. You don't even know if he's interested in you.*

I tried to stop my thoughts from racing ahead of me. I didn't want to get my hopes up. I'd met someone with whom everything had been implicit thus far, in terms of our connection. Maybe he wasn't even interested in me. Maybe this was all in my head. I got out of bed languorously, slipped on my caftan, and made my way into the living room. I decided to play some music. It had been a while since my apartment was filled with uplifting tunes, and I turned on the radio and tuned into a happy channel. Then, I went to the kitchen to make myself a cup of coffee. I was just about to settle down to read the newspapers and to see whether Tony had printed my article in the *Manhattan Times* on vertical gardens in the city, something which he'd promised to do, when my phone rang.

It was Devlin. First thing in the morning.

"Hi," he said, sounding somber. *What now?*

"Good morning," I said rather coldly. I didn't know why he was calling. Things were quite strained between us, and I assumed it had something to do with the divorce. Or maybe one of our children.

"Is everything okay with Lexie?" I asked.

"Oh, she's fine," he said, dismissing the thought.

"I called because ... I wanted to let you know something. Imogen, you can have fifty percent of everything in the divorce. Half of everything. I'm not going to contest it, not anymore. The joint properties. All of it. I don't want to fight over materialistic things like wealth anymore, and I don't want to drag our children into the middle of this. I'll remove the alcohol-abuse insinuations."

184

I was completely stunned. There was an interminably long moment of silence as I processed it all, and then I asked my soon-to-be ex-husband, Devlin, "Why the change of heart? What brought this largesse on? I don't understand. Until a few days ago, you were willing to fight me for everything."

It didn't add up with the person he had revealed himself to be. It didn't make sense.

"Like you don't know," he scoffed, sounding bitter, suddenly.

"What?" I asked, completely confused.

"Let's cut the crap, Imogen. I didn't think you'd stoop this low and use such tactics."

I was flummoxed. "I don't know what you're talking about, Devlin. Did something happen?"

Finally, he said, "Well, your crazy, new boyfriend paid me a visit. Late last night."

"My boyfriend?"

"Yes, your boyfriend. Brendan. The recently exonerated serial killer. The Wolfman. Please ask him to stay the hell away from me, alright? I'm giving you whatever you want. I don't want to be constantly looking over my shoulders, wondering if I'm going to be attacked by this mad person who, up until yesterday, was accused of murdering people. Just ask your nut-job of a boyfriend to stay away from me, Imogen!" Devlin was screaming on the phone!

I was stunned. I didn't know what to say.

"What happened?" I asked.

"You know exactly what happened. Let's not act out a farce here, okay? He scares me, Imogen, and I frankly don't know what you're doing with him. God knows what he's capable of, and I don't want to live with the fear of trying to figure that out. You do whatever you want with your life, you're a grown woman, but keep him away from me. Understand? I'll get the lawyers to draw up the new divorce papers. I've got to go. I'm running late for a meeting."

And without waiting for a response, Devlin hung up on the call. I sat in silence on my couch, my cellphone on my lap, and tried to process the insanity of what my husband had just shared with me. I realized two things, quickly. One, that Devlin was capable of being afraid, very, very afraid. Underneath that bravado, that arrogance, was a man who was desperately afraid of things. That it was all an act. Something about that gave me a lot of pleasure.

Second, I realized that Brendan had paid him a visit late last night and had said something to him, had threatened him in a manner that had made Devlin fear for his life. I do not condone violence of any kind. I'm not that sort of a person. And from Brendan, I had not sensed a vicious streak, not an iota of it. The aura that had emanated from him, and which my own Faerie nature had responded to, was one of goodness. So, I knew he was not capable of that kind of violence.

It then became clear to me that my feelings for Brendan were indeed reciprocated, that he had felt that visceral connection with me, too. After a long time, somebody had felt the need to stand up for me, to protect me. He might've gone about it in the wrong way, and perhaps I should've been offended that someone felt they had to fight my battles for me. That Brendan had taken such a liberty with me, and my personal space. But, the truth of the matter was, at that moment, I didn't feel offended at all. I feel pleased. Very pleased. I felt a warm glow inside at Brenden's display of chivalry.

I couldn't believe he'd done what he had done, but he pulled it off, and against all odds, the uphill battle that I was facing with my husband had disappeared. Just like that. There are things I would never openly admit: That I would be okay with threatening another person. No.

But deep inside, perhaps it was that visceral connection that I'd felt with Brendan that made me feel it was alright, at that particular moment. Or maybe, I am willing to admit, it was the intense attraction I felt for the man that seemed to justify the brazen act. But Brendan had wanted to protect me. And, not since Michael back in Scotland, had I felt a sense of being taken care of, truly so, by another man. I felt tears well up in my eyes. And a hot flush of attraction through my body. I was excited about how the day was going to unfold. I didn't know if I should pick up the phone and call Brendan. Should I even bring it up? Because I was pretty sure what he did was thoroughly illegal.

As if timed to perfection, and to answer my doubts, the doorbell rang. I opened it and there, standing in front of me, was Brendan. He looked at me expectantly. The moments that followed went by agonizingly slowly. I knew I should have mentioned what Devlin had just said on the phone. But I could see in his eyes that he knew that I knew You may find it hard to believe how the next few moments unfolded, but that visceral connection I keep referring to ... well, it was real.

Nothing was said. Brendan entered the apartment and shut the door behind him. And then, we were in each other's arms. It was unbridled passion. He lifted me up and carried me straight into the bedroom. He didn't wait to unbutton my shirt but ripped it off. I'd already wrapped my legs around his torso and hastily unbuttoned his shirt. And he did the rest for me. He pulled off his pants and yanked off my underwear. I clung to his lean and firm body as he thrust himself into me with a force I'd not anticipated. My body welcomed him. My body ached for him. The emotions that overwhelmed me are hard to explain. I felt as one with another human being for the first time in my life. Emotions were mixed up with the physicality of it all, and I felt a complete fusion of mind, body, and spirit. He kept loving me until I couldn't take the intensity of emotions anymore, and I cried out. Brendan cried out too. It was all over in a matter of minutes, and he lay on top of me, breathless.

I was utterly, completely vanquished, emotionally and physically, by this beautiful and mysterious man. We lay there breathless, our eyes closed, for several minutes. I felt an emotional release I hadn't experienced in a very long time. I'd felt the deepest connection with a man with whom I'd yet to color in all the details. I

188

still didn't know his whole story. He was still hiding, if only in words, his biggest secret. But, there would be a time for words. It wasn't at this moment.

He gently rolled over to the side and then held me tightly in his arms. I couldn't believe what had just happened, but at the same time, it also felt like the most natural thing in the world. Strange are the mysteries of the universe. We lay there for several minutes, not saying a word, our raspy breaths filling in the spaces between our tightly entwined bodies. Finally, I opened my mouth and asked him: "How long have you known, Brendan?"

There was a long pause and then he said, "How long have I known what?"

"That you were part man, part wolf?"

The room suddenly went very silent, as I almost stopped breathing, waiting for his response.

Then he turned me around in his arms, so we were facing each other, and said:

"How do you know these things about me? How do you know me so well? What is this connection we have? How did you know I was innocent? And how do you know this? About the wolf nature?"

I looked at him for a long moment, aching to share my story. But something in me still stopped me. Instead, I just said, "Do you trust me? Do you believe that I have my reasons for knowing? That I will share them with you when the time is right? Can you trust me enough to know that I know that you are good? And kind. I know of your supernatural nature. I know the agony and anguish you've been living in for years. The isolation you've felt, the torment at being separated from your parents. I understand it all. I know everything about you, the one question I can't answer is *how*. Not at this moment. But I will. I promise there will be a time when I will tell you everything. Do you trust me to believe that?"

"Can't you just tell me now? Brendan asked, looking deeply into my eyes while stroking my hair, and holding my body.

"I will soon," I said. "But can you just trust me, nevertheless?"

He stared into my eyes.

"You know of my innocence," he said. "And you're the only person in the world who knows of the animal side of me. My wolf nature. Lycanthropy? I read about it enough over the years, trying to find answers as to why I was behaving the way I was. The worst part was I couldn't tell anybody. I couldn't share my secret. People would think I was crazy," he said, his eyes welling up with tears. I pulled him close to me and held his head in my hands. Our bodies were completely entwined.

"I can feel your pain, Brendan. You don't have to hide anything anymore. You've found someone who understands. I need you to know that. You can tell me anything."

"Then, why can't you tell me everything?" he asked again. It was a fair question.

"I will soon," I promised. I didn't know how to explain to him that I was a mother, first and foremost. And a mother's instinct is to protect her children. I wasn't ready to share my secret with Brendan before I had told my own children.

I hadn't worked out that part yet. It seemed the time had come to share my past, truly share it, with those that loved me. I would. Right then, at that moment, lying in the arms of this man toward whom I felt a surge of emotion I hadn't experienced with any other man in my life, all I could bring myself to say was, "You're not alone anymore, Brendan. Whatever is to become of us, I promise you, you'll never be alone, anymore."

"What do you mean *what is to become of us?*" he asked, turning to face me. "I'm never letting you go," he said, simply.

"Oh, and do I have a say in this?" I asked him, playfully.

"No, not really," he answered, only half-joking.

And his response pleased me very much. There was nothing threatening about this beautiful man lying in my arms. He wanted to protect me, take care of me. He respected me. And even though we'd known each other only for a very short period of time, perhaps it was that visceral and metaphysical connection we shared. But within the boundaries of that metaphysical bond, nothing seemed off bounds.

"I don't want to lose you either," I said. "I've been lonely. And the last few months have been really hard. And then, I felt tears in my eyes. I hadn't realized what a toll the situation with Devlin had taken. It finally felt like I was in a safe space where I could express the grief that had built up inside for the demise of a life that I'd built carefully for twenty years. I burst out crying. It was his time to console me.

The day went by as we lay in each other's arms, crying and laughing. And making love. The words were spattered and intermittent. Brief glimpses into each other's long lives. But, it was beyond words, what we shared. And so, we expressed it physically. The whole night we made violent and passionate love. I didn't feel middle-aged that night. I feel young and vibrant. I felt renewed. Funnily enough, in my youth, I'd always been a bit reserved in the bedroom. But, simply because I'd felt so connected with this individual, nothing seemed inappropriate. I lost track of the number of times we made love that night. He was forceful, almost to the point of being violent, but I didn't mind. My body craved it. Years of damage and heartache, dating all the way back to my father's despicable behavior, and my husband's acts of infidelity, and my daughter's fecklessness, were sloughed off my body.

I felt reborn. I was connecting sexually and physically for the first time with another magical being, a spiritual being, and could feel years of heartache melting away. I knew I was a changed woman. I'd found true love. As Brendan held me protectively in his arms, his legs intertwined with mine, I knew the time would come where we would need to catch up with words, to the place where our hearts already were. Utterly and completely entwined with each other.

14

THE NEXT MORNING, as the faint rumblings and stirrings of traffic from outside could be heard, the light filtered into the room in a hazy glow. The reality of what had transpired over the last 24 hours started sinking in. I was free from my husband's shackles. I was, for all practical purposes, financially secure. And I had an incredible man entwined in my arms.

But there were the murders. Yes, the murders. And the perpetrator of those hideous crimes had not yet been caught. I still had a commitment to the NYPD, to Max and Alberto. My mind resisted the reality of it all, and I want to stay ensconced in the arms of this surreal being. But the threads of the day that were unfolding had already started pulling at my consciousness. I could feel Brendan stir next to me. I turned around and stared at him while his eyes were still closed.

"Do you like doing that?" he asked, and I was taken aback. I hadn't realized he had woken.

"Doing what?" I asked.

"Staring at people while they sleep?"

"Well, I don't mind it when the person is kind of good looking," offering his ego some salve.

He opened his eyes and smiled at me.

"I know you're full of questions," he said, almost as if reading my mind. "And I want to tell you everything, not just about the last twenty years of my life, but from even before, my childhood to my privileged upbringing to my so-called meltdown. To that period in hell and the psychiatric facility. And then to my years of ... my lost years," he said, summing it up, rather melancholically.

"But Imogen, I think we need to focus on the fact that we're here, in each other's arms. And that's something. Hope."

"I agree," I said emphatically.

"But if I'm to be honest, even in this moment of utter happiness, I'm filled with a certain anger."

I stayed quiet and listened.

"I know that my name, whatever that means at this point, was dragged through the mud by the killer, by this awful human being. Ripping women apart and murdering them for pleasure ... "

I wanted to see where he was going with this.

"I know people will say things will be okay, but I know for a fact that no one will probably ever look at me the same way, again.

And, these poor women. They deserve justice, their families deserve justice."

"I know, Brendan. I'm still committed to the NYPD to help solve this issue. I'm relieved you're off the hook. But I still feel entwined with the case. And I want to see things through. Your part in this is not over, I'm afraid," I said, stroking his face gently.

"You're the only one who's seen the face of the murderer. I think we need to go into the precinct today and you sit down with a sketch artist, and you pull up from your memory every detail that you can think of, from that fateful night."

"Yes," Brendan agreed. It was the right thing to do, and besides, that's what Max was probably going to ask him to do, anyway.

"Can you think of anything else about that night?" I asked him gently.

"He wore a thick coat. I remember his face, it was craggy and lean. I'd be better able to describe it to a sketch artist."

"Okay," I said, getting out of bed.

"Do you have to? " he asked, suggestively.

"Yes, it's time to face the day, Brendan," I said, smiling down at him.

He looked at my body. And then, he had a look of embarrassment on his face.

"Sorry," he said.

"What for?" I asked him, curiously.

"For all the bruises," he sheepishly said.

"Well, you are part-beast," I said. We both burst out laughing.

"Don't be sorry, Brandon. I *like* having you on me."

We stared at each other for a long moment, and then I went into the shower. Brendan followed me. This was something I'd never been comfortable with, in the long years of my marriage, taking a shower with my husband. But somehow, I felt completely at ease doing with Brendan. It seemed natural, in the intimacy that we shared.

Afterward, as expected, Brendan got a call from Detective Max, asking him to come down to the station. And before I could protest, Brendan said, "Imogen's with me. Can she come along too?"

I immediately squished up my face in protest. *Why did he say that?* Now, I was going to have to explain my presence with Brendan. Brendan looked assured of himself. But I couldn't bring myself to get angry. I could hear Max's voice through the phone. He sounded surprised. Naturally.

Brendan chuckled and said, "Yes, it's a long story. Imogen and I will explain. Tell us what time to come in?"

When Brendan hung up, I looked at him with mock seriousness.

"Why did you tell Max that you were with me?"

"Imogen, I don't want any more lies. Covering up and all of that. You've done nothing wrong. I was exonerated yesterday, before whatever happened between us happened."

196

"It's not that simple, Brendan," I said, looking frustrated. "I'm still associated with the case."

"Well, you were called in on a specific assignment, right? To see if you could figure me out? That assignment got over day-before-yesterday. At some point in time. Before we made passionate love," he said impishly.

"You're incorrigible!" I said, looking flabbergasted. "This is embarrassing for me. How am I going to explain myself? It's unprofessional."

"Well, what are you going to do, spend the rest of our lives keeping this a secret?"

I couldn't believe he was using expressions like the *rest of our lives*. But the funny thing was it felt completely natural when he said it.

"No, but I would have given it a period of time before proffering this recent development. You know, blur the edges a bit, keep them guessing, protect my reputation."

He looked at me perplexed.

"You really have no clue, do you?" I said, with a grin on my face, in response to which he swooped in to pick me up in his arms and lay me down on the couch.

"Oh, no," I said, squealing in delight, "it's not happening now, do you hear? I'm exhausted. My body needs to recuperate."

He smiled at me with a great deal of affection, and said, "Okay, you're off the hook. For now."

Brendan's face suddenly took on a somber hue.

"What happened?" I asked, collecting myself.

Brendan was lost in thought for a long moment. And then, a look of realization crossed his face. He got up urgently from the couch.

"Listen, Imogen, we're to meet Max at the station at eleven, right? Let me go home first. Given that I disappeared on my parents last night, again, I'm sure they must be a bit anxious, with my history. I know, I'm a forty-five-year-old man, but after what I've put them through, I owe them reassurance.

"You're not going to tell them about me, are you?" I asked, looking concerned.

"Not yet," he said, smiling. "Would it be wrong if I did?"

"Not yet, Brendan, not yet," I said.

"No, you see, I just thought of a plan," he said.

"A plan for what? I asked.

"How to catch the killer."

It felt as if the traffic outside had faded away and there was complete silence in the room as I listened intently.

"What's your plan?" I asked hesitantly.

To that, he smiled at me and said, "More shall be revealed at the police station. But I need to go ask my parents something first."

I was intrigued, but I let it slide. Brendan kissed me, said goodbye, and left the apartment.

I went and stood in front of the mirror on top of the credenza and stared at my body. I had bruises and marks on my neck and my arms. I looked like I had been battered. The truth was, I really was incredibly happy. It felt as if I were standing on the precipice of a cliff and was about to dive into new, uncharted territory. But I wasn't afraid. I was eager to get started.

But first, we had to solve a murder, a gruesome series of murders. *What was Brendan's plan?*

When I walked into the station, a little past eleven, ensuring I was wearing full sleeves and a scarf to cover up my neck, which looked like the relief map of a mountain range, I tried hard to avoid making eye contact with Max, who kept staring at me.

"Here she is," he said, loudly. "I thought you were coming in together with Brendan."

"No, I had to run an errand before coming in."

I smiled at Max, looking uncomfortably at my feet.

"Anyway," Max cleared his throat, "Brendan, we're really glad you're in the clear. Imogen was certain from the beginning that you were innocent, and it proved to be true. We're sorry for any difficulty we put you through."

Brendan smiled patiently.

"We thought we'd give you a day to rest up and enjoy your exoneration, so to speak, but now it's time to get to business. You said you saw the killer. We have a sketch artist lined up. He's ready to take details from you and maybe put together a profile. A composite of this person. I also want to sit down with you and talk at length about anything that you may remember about that night, about what you saw, what you heard, what you smelled. Anything really, that gives us clues?

"I'm happy to oblige, Detective Murphy, that's what I'm here for. I'm all yours today. But, I also want to suggest something," Brendan started.

Detective Murphy looked at him perplexed.

"Oh?"

"I know I'm probably jumping ahead of myself, and I don't know if it's my place to make such suggestions to the police, but I've just come from talking to my parents about it, and they were really against it at first, but they've reluctantly agreed to let me go ahead with it. With your assistance."

"What's this about?" Alberto asked, impatiently.

"I'd like to go on television. And make a public statement that I saw the face of the killer."

My heart sank utterly and completely.

"That's insane, Brendan."

"Hold on, darling," he said, at which Max looked at me utterly wide-eyed.

"Darling? Am I missing something?"

"Actually, yes. You are," Brendan said, "but we'll get to that later." Max stared at me for a long moment before turning back to face Brendan.

Alberto had a smile on his face that went from ear to ear. I felt my cheeks flush and was completely uncomfortable at being there. But I was alarmed at what I was hearing.

"My plan is that I go on television and tell the world that I did see the killer."

"It will make you a moving target," I blurted out loud.

Max took a deep breath and said, "She's right, Brendan. If you do that, whoever is out there—that person is very, very dangerous, and probably will come after you."

"I know," Brendan said. "I want him to."

"You can't do this," I protested.

"I think it's the only way to catch him soon. I mean, I can help you come up with a sketch of the person. But remember, it was dark. And these things aren't reliable beyond a point. And right now, we don't have any other forensic evidence, if I'm correct. Right?"

Max looked at him in tacit agreement.

"If I announce to the world that I saw the killer, it's a direct message to him. He clearly doesn't want to be found. I almost feel certain that he will come after me, and if you have me secretly followed by detectives or whatever, then you can catch him!"

"This is like something from a movie, Brendan. You can't do this," I said. "It's utterly reckless and insane and irresponsible. You've just been reunited with your parents. You can't put them through that, again."

"Hold on," Max said. "I mean, it is risky, that is obvious."

"Will you be willing to sign liability disclaimers and things like that, because we have a process for this kind of high-risk shit?" Alberto offered.

"Yes, I'll do whatever it takes, I want to catch this person. He's dragged me and my family's name through the mud. He's murdered innocent women. Bludgeoned them to death. He can't get away with it, and none of us, let's face it, are going to rest easy until he's found and held accountable."

"You're personally invested in this, I see that. But, what are your parents saying about this?" I asked, suddenly realizing that that's what he'd gone home—to talk to his parents about this plan.

"I can't believe that they would agree with it."

"Actually, Imogen, they've been through a lot over the last twenty years. It's changed them. And they're angry, too, about everything that the family has been through. And what this perpetrator has done. People think the rich don't care, but we're not all so bad. They were very reluctant about it first, but in the way only a child can convince his parents, I did manage to change their minds in the end. Although," Brendan said, turning to face the detectives, "my father has insisted that we also use our own personal security in the operation."

"What do you mean *insist?*" Max asked, annoyed.

"It means they agreed on the condition that you work in tandem with my father's personal security staff."

Alberto rolled his eyes. "They don't trust us."

"No offense, Detective, but for a period of time, you thought I was a serial killer, then proceeded to hold me with no evidence."

"You threatened to bite people in Central Park!"

"So they claimed. I did no such thing," Brendan held firm. "My parents insist on this, for their own reassurance, that everything is being done to protect me while I go ahead with this. I am offering myself to you, but these are the conditions. I hope you accept them."

Detectives Marx and Alberto exchanged a long look.

"We'll have to speak to our superiors, but this could very well be a plan. You still need to sit down with the sketch artist, though. And we need to have that discussion, too, to see if you can remember anything else."

"Sure, anything you want," Brendan said.

He turned to me and tried to reach for my arms, but I moved away, quickly. The detectives were staring at us. Both of us.

"Imogen," Brendan said softly so that only I would hear. "Maybe you need to take it easy for the rest of the day. Looks like I'm going to be tied up here."

"Yes, and why are you here?" Alberto asked, not in a rude manner, but playfully.

I realized the charade was over and looked at Max and said, "I'd like a minute to speak to you. In private. It can't wait."

"Okay," he said. I turned and looked at Brendan. Brendan smiled at me encouragingly.

I knew this was not going to be easy. It ended up being one of the most uncomfortable and difficult things I had to do. But I had to come clean to the NYPD, I had to let them know of the developments that had happened with Brendan. I knew what it meant. It meant that I would be off the case. I was okay with that.

Things had changed so drastically in the last day. Brendan had been cleared. He was the reason why I'd been called into the case in the first place. Also, I didn't need the job anymore, as it turned out. But there was my reputation, and it was going to take a body blow. But given what I'd experienced the night before and the connection that I'd now formed with this incredible, supernatural being, I knew there was truth in the saying: *you can't win them all*. Brendan was led by Alberto into the depths of the precinct, and as I saw his tall, lean body turn a corner and disappear, I realized that whatever loss of reputation I was going to suffer, or embarrassment I might be causing myself with Max, it was going to be worth it.

15

I COULDN'T BELIEVE how smoothly the whole lunch was going. Brendan and Lexie and Justin and no fireworks. And me. Of course. Did I forget to mention I was there? Introducing my son and daughter to a man who'd been recently vilified by the press, who was the center of attention at that restaurant, most certainly, and who, for some reason, was having none of the torment I was, interacting with my kids.

"So, Justin, I'm to gather you're pursuing dreams of being a medical doctor?" Brendan tried to engage my son, who responded the way I'd brought him up to – politely.

"Yeah. I mean, it was always Mum's goal, and I wanted to honor the dreams she couldn't live out."

I loved Justin. Kind and considerate, as always.

"And what do you plan on specializing in?" Brendan asked him.

"Surgery. Like Mum had wanted to," he said, looking at me, eager to please.

"And Lexie? What are your plans?" Brendan asked my disengaged daughter who'd expressed no interest in the lunch and had treated the entire affair as an obligation. It had been an uphill task convincing her to meet me after our last encounter, but I knew she wouldn't be able to resist meeting Brendan, a celebrity at this point.

"Oh, I don't know. Community college isn't Yale. But I'm sure I'll land on my feet somewhere."

"But you must have dreams?" Brendan persisted. "Plans?"

"Why? Maybe I just want to be a drifter. Surely, that's something you can empathize with," she said, staring at Brendan.

I felt my heart sink. It was one thing to take pot-shots at me, another to mock the sensitive aspects of another person's trying life story. That bitterness. Where was she getting it from?

"That's enough, Lexie," I said sternly, staring at my daughter.

"Oh, it's okay," Brendan said.

He just smiled and shrugged it off. The late January light filtered in sharply through the windows of the restaurant, and I was counting the seconds till this lunch would be over, already.

I knew I had to introduce my kids to Brendan at some point, sooner or later. I would've preferred later. But Brendan had insisted when he found out the kids were coming home for the weekend. It was a special occasion. It was Justin's birthday today.

"Happy birthday, Justin," I said with a big smile when the cake had been brought out and everyone gathered around to blow out the candles. There was a smattering of people at the restaurant and quite a few curious onlookers. In the few weeks since Brendan had been released, people would recognize him on the streets and since we were spending a lot of time together, we'd made the gossip columns. It's amazing how quickly the human mind adjusts to situations, however bizarre.

But we'd been so wrapped up in each other, that we looked at it as a small price to pay, for being able to be together.

"May I ask you a question?" Alexis turned to face Brendan when we'd settled back down in our chairs.

"Sure," he said while munching on his salad.

"In the press conference two weeks ago, you'd said you saw the face of the killer?"

"Lexie, you know he can't discuss the case ... " I started, getting annoyed at my daughter, but she quickly continued.

" ... You'd said you had been off your meds for a really long time. And that that was what had prompted your breakdown and unusual behavior, living in the park all those years ... "

Brendan stared at her blankly.

"I guess I want to know how you can be considered a credible witness? How can the cops, or anyone trust what you saw, or claim to have seen?"

"Lexie, why don't you just shut and focus on your meal?" Justin said to his sister.

"No, no it's alright," Brendan began.

"Brendan, you don't have to answer my daughter … "

"Well Lexie, you know I can't discuss the specifics of the case? But you're right. Everything I say will be subject to scrutiny and taken with a healthy dose of skepticism. But I'm all the lead they've got at the moment. And now that I'm back on my meds and am seeing things a lot more clearly, I still stand by what or whom I saw that fateful night. I know what I saw. And the cops will follow through on all leads."

"Okay," she said, suddenly looking disinterested, again, picking up her cell phone and staring at the screen.

I looked at Brendan apologetically, but he smiled at me, reassuringly.

"The thing is, Lexie," he continued, "all we have at the end of the day is our inner voice and conscience telling us what's right or wrong. Even people who struggle with mental health issues, they are real, sentient beings, with emotions and feelings, and need to be treated with care and consideration."

"Whatever," she said, unimpressed.

"Do you think some people matter more than others?" he pressed. "That all humans don't deserve to be treated fairly and with equal love and respect?"

I felt the conversation slipping away.

"I know some voices are more important than others. It isn't a fair world. Look around you, for god's sake. I know you've been ... in seclusion for a while, but, in the real world, yes, some people matter more than others."

"The real world? What do you know of the real world, Lexie? You're a spoiled Daddy's girl, with all your expenses being taken care of, and with no purpose or direction in your life," Justin offered, scornfully. This led to another huge argument between siblings, and I didn't have the energy to interject. My mind had already started drifting when Lexie had brought up the press conference.

I nervously glanced around the restaurant. Nothing seemed out of place, except for the fact that, of course, a few tables away, were unobtrusively seated, a small contingency of NYPD detectives and private security guards, in casual clothes pretending to be customers, keeping a constant eye on Brendan. Their presence reassured me immensely, but I still couldn't shake off the feeling that he was vulnerable.

The kids went over to their father's place after lunch, and Brendan and I went back to my apartment. Life had changed so dramatically in the last few weeks. So much had happened. Yet, nothing felt too rushed for me. I was in love, truly, consummately, in love. My financial and legal situation with Devlin had changed overnight, and I felt more secure about my future than I had in a really long time. So, even though there was danger, visceral danger lurking around every turn, with a violent predator on the loose and, in all probability, targeting my boyfriend, I'd felt a sense of contentment and was overcome with the feeling that life was moving forward, and positively. Justin called to say he and Lexie would be staying over at their father's, and I was okay with that. The truth was, with Brendan in constant danger, my instinct was to keep my children safe, as well. Them being further away was a good thing.

Brendan's needs in these early days of him adjusting back to normal life were simple. He wanted to be around me all the time, and I was okay with that. I'd been introduced to his parents, formally, as the girl he was seeing, and awkward as that was, given the circumstances in which we'd met, it soon became apparent to me that all Brendan's parents wanted was to see their son happy. And he was happy with me. And so, they graciously tolerated me.

In the apartment, Brendan was on the couch watching the news eagerly for any updates on our case and I lay in his lap, reading a book. I could get used to this life, I told myself, knowing full-well this situation we were in, this bubble, was temporary. At some point, the case hopefully would be solved and Brendan could get on with the business of actually resuming his life. He still had many, many good years ahead of him. What did he want to do with them? He had to figure out basic things that people worked out at a much earlier stage in their lives, but on the advice of a therapist whom he'd agreed to meet, it was suggested that we all take things slowly, and let him get adjusted to normal life again.

Normal. Would anything ever be normal for him, again? He'd had such an unusual life thus far. And would continue to remain different permanently due to his lycanthropy. But now, he had me on his side. A partner who knew his secret. He was not alone anymore. And this knowledge gave him immense strength. And for this, he was extremely grateful toward me. It reflected in the little things he did for me, tiny acts of caring and consideration, and it also reflected in the intimacy we shared.

The truth was, I was a forty-three-year-old woman and in the past few weeks had had more sex than I'd probably had in years of my marriage! His yearning for me was constant and relentless, and I didn't mind, but something had happened a few nights ago that'd got me to start questioning the nature of his supernatural powers. What they entailed? What set them off? And how or whether they could be controlled? The thing about Brendan was that he'd spent so much time hiding from his true nature, and being ashamed of it, that he'd not spent a lot of time understanding this overwhelming force that coursed through his veins. Maybe the more he figured out how it worked, and understood its full potential, for better or worse, he would feel more comfortable with that part of himself.

I understood the irony of my own thoughts. I was a faerie and yet, had also hid it from those I was closest to, in my life in America. Even Brendan and my own kids had no idea about this core nature of mine. But the difference was, I'd always known the full force of my powers, its strengths, and limitations, and had had the ability, in my youth, to share it with other kindred spirits, back in Scotland. I'd had a community, and that's made all the difference. I knew Brendan was different from me in his supernatural gift, his was more powerful and dangerous, and I'd got my first glimpse into it when we were making love a few nights back.

It was passionate as always and intense. Too intense. And then, I felt it. The beginnings of him changing. As he lay there, above me, Brendan's eyes glazed over to a brighter, lighter shade of intense blue, and the animal in him started surfacing. His teeth visibly sharpened and the coarse hair on his body thickened. The change was imperceptible but palpable, and I immediately pulled away, a little frightened.

"I'm sorry, I'm sorry," he said, looking upset and shaken. "This was what I was afraid of," he whispered, staring into my eyes with despair.

"You were going through the change, weren't you?" I asked, but it wasn't really a question. I'd wanted to talk about this part of him for a while now, and unexpectedly, the opportunity had presented itself.

He nodded in my direction. "I have to be careful, Imogen. That part of me, it's not something I allow to surface, not if I can help it, but it inevitably does, in moments of agitation."

"Or passion," I added, sympathetically.

"Yes. Passion. Also, under a full moon. And it's almost like I need to allow the beast in me to surface, periodically, or it finds ways to come to the fore at the most inopportune moments. The past few weeks, I've been surrounded by all of you, the media, cops, security personnel. I haven't had the space to let this happen."

"No, I get it," I said. "You need to let the wolf part of your persona surface, from time to time, or it gets out of control," I said, reaching out for him, but he'd moved away.

"How am I going to allow this to happen, Imogen?" he asked, looking at me worriedly. "My parents can't ever find out. I'm in the center of this media storm."

"That will die down, Brendan," I offered. "As for the animal in you surfacing ... do you think that side of you is dangerous?" I asked.

"Not toward you," he reassured me. "Never."

"Then, I propose you allow it to happen around me. In this safe space."

"It's frightening to go through, much less witness. So little is in my control, when it happens. I'd be too embarrassed."

"Brendan, it's this shame that you've felt for so long, that made you hide in the park for twenty years. You've missed out on so much. Don't miss out on the rest. For my part, I promise you it won't change how I see you."

"How could it not?"

I wanted to tell him, *Because I'm a supernatural being, too*, but I just stared at him and said, "Because what I feel for you is true love. You're my soulmate. And when you've found true love, nothing colors how you see that person. Besides, I love everything about you, and that means I love the wolf inside you, too."

"Really?" he asked, searching for reassurance.

"Yes. Really. Use this apartment as your safe space. When you need to ... change ... do it here. And if you don't want me around, I can step out, or be in the other room. We will face this together. And in no time, we'll imbibe it into our lives as just another aspect to our existence."

He stared at me with searing intensity, then said, "Well, I'd like to try and get back to doing what we were doing, but I'm pretty sure that part of me will surface tonight, if I do."

I stared at him for a very long and silent moment.

"I'm not afraid. I want you tonight. I want all of you, every part. I trust you, Brendan. I love you," I said, simply.

Brendan came over to me and pulled me close in a tight embrace. And as we made love, I experienced the strangest, most visceral, and beautiful experience I had in my life. It was right up there with giving birth to my children. Brendan transformed into a werewolf as we made love, but we stayed tied together, our limbs intertwined, his body in mine, and with my eyes closed, I could sense his animal energy coursing through my racing blood. It was not scary, it was sacred and wonderful and spiritual.

When we were done and lay spent in each other's arms, he transitioned back to human, and I observed him go through the change. It was fascinating. And endearing. To think that he'd had to carry this profound, body-altering secret with him for years, decades, and the loneliness he must have felt as a result, moved me. I stroked his face gently with my fingers, as we lay facing each other on the bed.

Brendan noticed the pendant on my necklace. The jade locket. He tried to open it and for a second, in my languorous reverie, I'd almost allowed him to do so. I suddenly came to my senses, and screamed, "No!" as I pulled the locket away from his fingers. He sat up on the bed and stared at me curiously.

I got up as well, with my fingers firmly wrapped around the unopened locket the witch had given me in Scotland, when I was a teenager, and look flustered.

"I'm sorry," I said. "I didn't mean to shout."

"Is there something you want to tell me, Imogen?" Brendan asked, referring to my reaction.

"It's nothing," I said, quickly.

"It's not nothing. A special gift from someone? An heirloom?"

"It's really nothing," I didn't want to talk about it.

"C'mon, I've been so frank with you about everything. My deepest, darkest secrets tonight. Can't you trust me?" he asked, almost playfully, lying back down on the bed.

I lay down beside him, took his arm, and covered my body with it. We lay there for a long moment in silence. I realized I didn't really need to lie about the locket.

"It was a gift. From a witch. Back in Killin. She told me never to open it, unless I was in mortal danger."

"A witch?"

"Yup."

"Are there really such people?"

"This I coming from a werewolf?" I asked, looking at him impishly.

"Fair enough."

"It was given to me just before I'd left Scotland. I don't know, I never opened it."

"So, you don't know what's on the inside?"

"No."

"Aren't you curious?"

"Not really. I'd be much more interested in testing out it's efficacy at a truly scary moment in my life, when I have nothing to lose!"

"I suppose that makes sense."

"You know, you're a complete enigma, Imogen McLelland," Brendan finally said, pulling me close to him.

"Why do you say that?"

"In these few weeks together, I've found you to be one of the most grounded, down-to-earth people I've ever met. And yet, you moonlight for the NYPD as a psychic! And you believe in the prophecy of witches from Scotland who've given you strange lockets."

"Can't I be a bit of both?" I asked facetiously.

"You can be whatever you want. But, I think there's a lot more to you than you're letting on. And I intend to find everything out."

"Oh really?" I said.

"Really," he echoed, throwing down the gauntlet.

"I mean, you never talk of your life in Scotland," he continued. He was in the mood to talk.

"I told you what happened there," I said, feeling that constriction in my throat that often surfaced at the mention of my childhood.

"I know this is a delicate subject for you – I mean, I clearly have sensed that over the past month—but, Imogen, don't you wish to see your parents again?"

The words sank to the pit of my stomach. It was a part of my brain I didn't want to visit, not on a beautiful night, entwined in my lover's arms. Eoin's face, and what he'd said to me about my sick mother, briefly flashed in my mind's eye. I blocked it out. It was too much.

"I'm not trying to pick a fight here, Imogen, but don't you think it's unfair? You want to help me, and have me open up about my deepest, darkest secrets, and yet, you clam up whenever I ask you valid questions, because I care. About your past. Your youth. About how you know so much about me when nobody else has a clue about the lycanthropy. About my innocence."

"I can't talk about it now, alright," I said sternly, and immediately, regretted the tone of my voice.

"Fine," Brendan said, getting out of bed and putting on his clothes.

"Where are you going?" I asked.

"I'm going to spend the night at home. I've just got back, and I've pretty much spent all my nights with you. I should probably spend some time with my parents," he said, ruefully.

"Please don't be mad at me," I pleaded. "I just need a little more time," I offered.

He turned around, looking at me a little wearily, and finally smiled. "You take the time you need, Imogen. But don't take forever."

With that, he kissed me and left the apartment.

Well, that was that, I said to myself, collapsing back on the bed, frustrated. I knew in my heart I had to come clean to Brendan. To my kids. I had to confront the matter that had brought Eoin all the way to NYC from Scotland. The matter being my aging and ailing mother. I thought of the rolling hills of Killin. I had a sudden flashback. I was lying in the meadows by the river in Michael's arms in the Scottish countryside, and the feeling of carefreeness that overcame me for an instant was like a jolt of lightning to my system. I quickly shook myself out of my reverie. Some memories were too profound, too damaging to be dealt with. And so, I had not confronted my past in nearly twenty years. But I realized, at that moment, that the past was catching up to me finally. This had been clear, in the way my life had played out the last few weeks. With Eoin's visit. With Brendan entering my life. The NYPD job. The troubling behavior of my daughter.

I finally realized that I had no alternative but to consciously start dealing with my childhood and my past, one frayed thread at a time, so I could weave together all the open-ended narratives that I'd left dangling and incomplete, simply because I'd been too much of a coward and too selfish in my youth, to cope with the various traumas.

But I was not a young girl anymore. I was a grown woman. I knew exactly who I was. And perhaps it was time, after all, that I started trusting the people I was closest to, with my own secrets, lest I ran the risk of losing it all, again.

I met with my physician, finally, an appointment I'd put off for weeks, in light of all the new developments in my life. The terrible dreams had stopped but the night sweats hadn't. What I'd assumed to be a result of the dreams had turned out to be a separate thing altogether. Peri-menopause. Here I was, feeling young and vigorous again, having great sex and enjoying all the giddy perks of a young romance as a middle-aged woman, but time had caught up to me. It was official. I was in the very early stages of going through "the change." Brendan was very understanding of the embarrassing, wet bed sheets at night, and was tolerant of me coming to terms with it all, but I needed some time with a female companion. To vent.

16

"I FEEL LIKE THIS IS DÉJÀ VU," Bonnie said, wryly, as we were back at the same restaurant where we'd last met, and when I'd drunk too much and had bitterly complained about the state of my crumbling marriage. How things had dramatically changed in the last few weeks since I'd met my best friend. The man who'd preoccupied my thoughts at the time, Devlin, was nowhere in the picture, and I'd a new boyfriend. A man who'd been suspected of being a serial killer and who was still at the center of much attention in Manhattan. He was a billionaire's son and dashingly handsome. I was moonlighting for the NYPD as a psychic. Understandably, Bonnie was full of questions, and she was a hard sell for my concocted stories, especially about the psychic business, so I knew I had to approach the evening carefully. Be smart about it. Except, the truth of the matter was, I'd no idea how to go about doing this. Not a clue.

"Bonnie, I'm so sorry I've not been in touch the past few weeks. It's been crazy at my end," I offered, apologetically.

"Clearly," she said, staring at me expectantly.

"Well, okay. You do deserve a good explanation for it all,' I said.

"I do," she added, flatly, a hint of a smile on her lips.

"So, I'm dating someone ... " I said.

"No kidding," she said.

"Oh Bonnie, it all happened so fast! And then, there was the new job with the NYPD. And things were a mess over Christmas with Devlin and that bitch of a new girlfriend! I emptied a bottle of wine on his head, Bonnie! And then, Alexis has been breaking my heart. And all the media attention, and ... "

"Whoa, whoa, hold on their, darling! I know a lot has happened. Take a big sip of that wine, simmer down, and then, start at the beginning. But wait. First tell me. How is he?"

"Who?"

"Oh, for fuck's sake! Brendan Connor! *The* Brendan Connor!"

"Oh, Bonnie, he is amazing!"

"You mean, in bed, right?"

"Bonnie!" I chided my friend, my cheeks blushing a crimson hue.

"That good, eh?" she said, and we both giggled uncontrollably.

"Okay, okay, now start at the beginning," she said, the tension having been dissipated.

"Oh, I don't know where to begin. Well, you knew about the divorce ... "

And so I told my friend everything. Well, almost everything. Bonnie didn't know about my Faerie life, naturally, and so I gave her as much of an update as I could, without veering into the territory of willfully lying to my best friend.

"But wait, Im, what is this business about being a psychic?" she stared at me imploringly.

"I've known you for ten years. Not once, not once have you ever mentioned anything of the sort. And then, suddenly, you're moonlighting for the NYPD in that capacity?"

I knew that was going to be an uphill battle. I hated that I had to lie to my friend. But I wasn't doing it out of pleasure. What choice did I have? My own children didn't know of their Faerie heritage? How could I tell Bonnie? And then, there was the visceral fear of losing her, when she'd discover I'd lied to her, or at least, hid a part of myself that was fundamental to me, for so long. I didn't want to jeopardize my friendship. What was I to do?

I finally decided to follow a middle at point-blank

"Bonnie. Do you trust me?" I asked her point-blank.

She was startled for a moment.

"Yes, of course, Im."

"Then, if I ask you to do something for me, will you do it? Which is just believe me when I say I have my reasons for not being able to tell you everything. I know you've always found my reticence over my childhood in Scotland frustrating, but what if I were to tell you, it's directly tied-in with this job that came up at the NYPD?"

Bonnie looked flustered. "Okay ... " she said, indicating that I continue.

"Well, I know you know I'm not a psychic, okay? That much is apparent. But, well, this job opportunity required that I present a front—a cover—for my real services."

"Which are ... ?" she asked.

"I can't tell you that," I said, flatly. What more could I say?

"Im, I love you. And I do trust you. But there's a limit to how much of a double-life you can lead."

"Excuse me?" I said, stung.

"For ten years, I've asked you about Scotland. Hardly a word on the subject was offered. And now, you're dating a man, whom you say you met on the job? And a man who's admitted to having serious mental health issues on national television, and who was a prime suspect in a serial-killer case up until a few weeks ago!"

"He's innocent, Bonnie," I said, sullenly.

"I mean, surely you can understand, as someone who loves you dearly, why all this might seem bit ... "

"A bit what?" I asked, defiantly.

"A bit alarming," she finally offered.

"I'm just worried for you. That maybe this divorce with Devlin has taken a toll on you. And you haven't been on your own for a long time. Maybe you're afraid of that?" she added

Bonnie's underestimation of me was indeed hurtful, but I also knew she was only doing so because she had so little of the truth to work with. This was my fault, and I wasn't going to take it out on a friend who'd been there for me through thick and thin.

"I'm not weak, Bonnie. I am truly in love. And when you meet Brendan, and see him for the wonderful person that he is, you'll feel better about all of this."

I took a deep breath. "You're right. I won't deny that I've hid a part of my life, my past from you, from the very beginning. But I just need you to trust me when I say I have good reasons for doing it. For both of us and our friendship. It's nothing sinister, I assure you. And I believe there will be a day when I can speak openly about it. And when I can, you will be the first non-family member I will discuss it all with. But for now, I'm just asking you to put your faith in me."

Bonnie stared at me patiently, took a long and defeated breath, and finally said, "Even the kids don't know?"

"No one. Not Devlin. Not the kids."

"And Brendan Connor? Does he know your secret?"

"No," I answered, truthfully.

"Okay," she finally said.

"Whatever it is, I know you must have your reasons. Now, tell me about the emptying of the red wine on that idiot's head, again." she said, with the hint of a naughty smile on her face, and we both laughed out loud.

"Oh, it was so worth it, Bonnie! You should have seen the look on his face!"

"Priceless!" she said, and everything was back to normal with us, at least for now.

"But seriously, Bonnie, I'm really worried about Lexie. She's acting difficult these days. Really difficult. I'm worried there's something bad going on with her," I confided in my best friend.

"How do you mean?" she asked.

"For starters, she took her father's side over our split. I mean she didn't explicitly spell it out, but she actually sided with him over me, during Christmas. We had a serious talk a few days later, and she said some things. Troubling things. I know we're supposed to be our children's biggest champions and think the best of them, but is it wrong as parents to notice when they're taking a wrong turn in life? You know, so we can try and stop them from hurting themselves?"

"Of course not. They might be our kids, but they're still human. It's worse to pretend the problem doesn't exist."

"But what if it's not a problem so much as ... a personality trait, I'm observing?"

"Such as?" Bonnie asked, leaning forward with her elbows on the table.

"I feel she's growing up to be a manipulative and privileged brat, frankly."

"Im, now come on ... "

"No, it's true. I see it. She's sided with her dad on the divorce, and that's because she sees him as being in a better financial place than me. She's thoughtless, generally, towards other people, and insensitive. And constantly taking digs at me. Hurtful digs," I vented, taking a sip of my wine.

"They're all like that! Kids! Passive-aggressive toward their parents, it's their God-given purpose I sometimes feel," she added. "Don't take it to heart, Im, I'm sure she'll outgrow it."

"Bonnie, she actually took digs at me in front of Devlin's new girlfriend. It was heartbreaking to see such behavior. It was cruel."

"I can't imagine how hard that must have been. Do you want me to talk to her?"

"Aunt Bonnie? Why not?" I said, smiling at my friend.

Bonnie looked out at the traffic on the streets for a moment and then turned to me and said, "You know, Im, I know it's not my place to suggest this, and I'm not trying to upset you here ... But has it ever occurred to you that this part of you that you keep to yourself, affects those surrounding you, even if that isn't your intent?"

"How do you mean?" I asked.

"Think about it. I've known you've kept a part of your life away from me since when I met you, and I'm just your friend! Don't you think your own flesh and blood have sense that distance as well? Your kids barely know about your childhood, Scotland, their grandparents. Do you think that it's this distance that Lexie's acting out against, in passive-aggressive ways? Kids are very intuitive.

226

Maybe she feels you are keeping a part of yourself away from her because you don't love her enough."

"That's ridiculous. I love both my kids to death," I added, getting upset.

"No, I know that. But sometimes children attribute reasons for our behavior. This secret your carrying, Im. Maybe it's time you told your family. Maybe this is the universe's way of telling you to wake up and smell the coffee."

Bonnie's words resonated with me the whole ride back home on the cab. Perhaps this was the time to share my secret with my children. It also meant I could open up, finally, to Brendan, something I was longing to do. Yearning to do. I was already deciding on when I was going to do this, and what my words would be to my kids, when I exited the cab, and quite literally, in a matter of seconds, the sensation overwhelmed me. That I was very, very close to danger. I turned swiftly around, even as the night air enveloped me in its cold clasp. It was night, although the street lights were brightly lit and the road was buzzing with the dredges of traffic. I looked all around me. There was a smattering of pedestrians, and my doorman was present a few feet away, but nothing stood out.

But I definitely felt it. The presence of evil. It was palpable. To my utter shock, the jade locket, for the first time in the twenty years I'd worn it, started radiating a dull glow, and I could feel heat emanating from it. I made straight for my building's door, and I ran inside. The doorman stared at me for my brusqueness, but I was overcome with the sensation of danger right next to me, then behind me, and the heat from the pendant warmed the skin between my breasts. I pressed the elevator button and waited impatiently for the lift to reach my floor. When I finally entered the elevator, there was no one else there, but the feeling of danger close to me hadn't abated. It was still close, and my hands were shaking and my heart racing, as I hastily opened the door to my apartment and slid inside. I leaned against the back of the door, in the darkened interiors of my apartment, in complete silence, with only the sound of my racing heartbeat in my ears, keeping me company. The danger was there, but not as close. For a moment it stayed the same, and then, the sensation slowly started receding.

I stood there in silence as the locket gradually started feeling less warm against the skin of my chest. I looked down at it, and it had almost stopped emanating heat and light. The sense of danger in the atmosphere receded. I turned on all the lights and sat down on the couch, completely shaken, sweat having beaded into little drops of moisture on my forehead, and in the clammy palms of my hands. I hadn't seen the killer, but he had been there. Watching me. And had followed me.

It had to be him. The killer had been close to me. Very close. Max had suggested that a security detail be given to me as well, but I'd brushed aside the notion. Brendan was staying with his parents that night. I thought of calling him but decided against alarming him.

I fished out my cell phone from my handbag and made a call.

228

"Max. Hi. It's me. Sorry to call so late," I said.

"No problem. Is everything okay?" he asked.

"That security detail you thought I could use? Would it be okay if I changed my mind on that? Yeah. I think I might be in need of protection," I offered, my voice still quivering.

"Oh god. Did something happen?" Max asked, instantly alarmed.

"You're the one person I can share this with. I sensed his presence near me, Max. Tonight. Just now. On the street. I didn't see him, but he was there."

"Jesus, Im. I'm getting you a twenty-four hour security detail right now. Stay inside and lock the doors, " he said.

"Yeah, okay. Thank you, Max," I said feebly, hanging up.

The locket had glowed for the first time in twenty years. The witch had spoken the truth. Things were coming to a head. I thought of my children and the danger I'd inadvertently exposed them to a few days ago, and started crying uncontrollably. It was time I told them everything. The time for secrets was over. Who knew how long we all had on this planet, and life was too short to be lived in the shadows. I thought of my mother back in Scotland and cried some more.

17

THE NEXT FEW WEEKS WENT BY IN A BLUR. I alternated between the extremes of domestic bliss with Brendan and the constant feeling that terror lurked just around the corner. Brendan spent most of his time with me, and the occasional evening at home with his parents. He'd realized at some point that it was probably best not to push me into talking about my life in Scotland, and I knew better than to ask him what his plans were for the future. His future. Our future. For, in Brendan, I knew implicitly I'd met the man with whom I was to spend the rest of my life. I hovered over him protectively, when we stepped out of the apartment, which wasn't really very often, and glowered at people who stared at him for too long. It was only a matter of time before Brendan connected the dots, though I'd warned Max from telling him about feeling physically threatened that evening he found out anyway, and

Brendan wouldn't let me out of his sight, as a result. We did everything as a unit, and I was pretty sure, all of Manhattan had come to know of the strange psychic who'd wheedled her way into the heart of an even stranger billionaire. We were an oddity, and so the news kept reporting on us, despite my fervid hopes that this sort of yellow journalism would stop after Brendan had been exonerated.

We were followed by the paparazzi to restaurants, to grocery stores, and even to the gym. It was thus a natural instinct to want to stay curled up within the warm confines of my apartment. We were in our own private universe, but I had to keep reminding myself that danger lurked just around the corner, and that Brendan was a marked man. I didn't want my children to come and visit me in this environment of uncertainty and danger, and also, the fact that the journalists were hounding us, made me extra-protective of my children's privacy. They'd asked for no part in this situation.

But, I'd made up my mind, as the days turned to weeks, and February had morphed into early March, that I would come clean about my Faerie heritage to my kids. Their heritage. That I would do this over spring break, which, to my surprise, both Alexia and Justin had decided to spend with their parents. Justin would stay with me, and Lexie with her dad. Justin needed to prepare for the MCATs and was using the break to do just that, and Lexie had nowhere particular to be, and so, had decided to come home. She'd rented an apartment next to her campus, and despite my best efforts to get her to take up a part-time job to get her hands dirty, she seemed intent, for all practical purposes, on increasing her social media presence. I'd thought my newfound notoriety would put my daughter off, but instead, she was using it as a vehicle to get more people to follow her. It enraged me, but Brendan had advised me to let it go. That it would only further deteriorate things between us if I'd pulled her up for it.

Brendan's sketch of the killer had been well-circulated in the press for weeks now, but there were no credible tugs on the line. Every lead had petered out to the complete frustration of the NYPD. The killer had been meticulously clean. He'd left no traces of hair or fiber or bodily secretion on the crime scene and on the victims. Strangely, not even in the bite marks. It made the detectives speculate on whether this had indeed been two of a series of murders. Because he seemed professional in his work. Thorough. He knew how not to get caught. Which made me worry endlessly about Brendan.

Brendan had refused to be cowed down by the killer and was relishing his newfound life every bit, making himself very exposed. Though this was part of the plan, and he was being protected by two sets of security personnel, round the clock, I still couldn't help but let my mind wander to the fact that this killer had been two steps ahead of us the entire time. That he was cunning and smart and knew how to stay hidden. I knew he'd been there outside the building that fateful evening, after my dinner with Bonnie, but I couldn't spot him. I hadn't sensed his presence like that since that evening, but I kept looking over my shoulders wherever I went. Being paranoid was another way of saying I was being cautious, and I didn't mind the label if it meant I was being extra careful.

I'd grown to recognize and become familiar with the protective, undercover entourage that followed Brendan and me wherever we went. The only places that were out of bounds for them were my apartment and Brendan's parents' home. They dutifully waited outside as we went on with the business of living our lives as normally as possible. Brendan was a man possessed. He was determined to solve this crime, even if the police couldn't, and had sheaves of paper, newspaper clippings, and notes and photographs, all strewn on my dining table, and which he poured over endlessly.

"Come on, Brendan, haven't you been over these things, enough?" I protested one evening in early March. "It's so macabre, morbid even. There are detectives on the case, this is their job. Why don't we ... nevermind ... " I said, abruptly.

Brendan looked up from the table and stared at me. "Nevermind what?" he asked.

"Okay. Well I was going to wait to bring this up with you, but I wanted to ask you if you'd thought about what you wanted to do?"

"What I want to do?" he repeated my words.

"Well, yes. With your life, I mean?"

He stared at me for a long moment.

"Actually, I have been thinking about it these days."

"Oh, that's great!" I said.

"Is it important for you that I worked?" he asked, suddenly.

"What? No. I didn't say that. It's just that, well, most people ... need to work," I stated bluntly.

"I've been through a lot, Imogen. It's messed up my view of the world. I'm not sure I'm cut out for the corporate world, not anymore."

"What are you leaning towards?" I asked him, carefully, not wanting to appear pushy. The truth was, in the brief time that I'd been with Brendan, I found him to be one of the most intense and driven people I'd ever met. Whatever he put his mind to, he did it with complete dedication and focus, almost to the point of an obsession. I personally didn't care if he ended up a carpenter or a corporate businessman, but I'd had enough experience with men like him to know they were never satisfied unless fully engaged. I'd thought the corporate world would be a great fit for him, simply because he'd wanted to be in that space as a young man, he had the personality and drive for it, and because I secretly felt it would make his parents, especially his father, very happy. Though Nancy and Frank Connor had never really warmed up to me, they tolerated me for their son. It was clear they doted on him, and though they'd kept a distance from me, I'd felt a great deal of empathy for them.

Their only son, presumed dead for twenty years, and with whom things had been left on a terrible note, was back in their lives, as if by magic, and they deserved some joy in their lives at long last. But it was clear that the relationship dynamics between parents and son were complex here, and this had not been helped by the separation. There was deep, abiding love beneath the surface, that was for certain, but there was also bitterness, and anger, and unspoken sentiments that'd been bottled up for far too long.

Further, I was the last person who could bring any of this up with Brendan because, frankly, I lacked credibility on this front. Who was I to offer advice on a subject in which I had my own demons to deal with?

"I have some ideas. I'm not certain yet, and until I am, of a plan, I don't really want to discuss it, Im. I hope that's okay?" he said, looking at me solicitously.

"Of course," I said, although I did feel a little hurt. But then, who was I to complain? I'd kept the biggest secret from him, and he knew this about me. Too many things were being left unsaid.

"I'm looking forward to the kids' visit," I said.

"Yes, I'd imagine having them around must fill you with a kind of joy I'll never experience," he abruptly said. This completely threw me.

"Don't say that, Brendan," I offered, immediately going over to his side.

"Oh, it's okay. I'm not complaining. But let's face it, I'm 46. I'm probably not going to be a father in this lifetime. And that's okay," he said.

I felt a profound sadness for this beautiful man. In the time we'd spent together, I'd never asked him about this. It'd never come up. And now, I could see, from the expression on his face and from the words unsaid, that this was something he would have wanted for himself.

"It's not too late," I offered, smiling. "I mean, I'm getting on in years, but you could always find yourself a pretty, young thing and have a ton of babies," I playfully said, stroking his hair.

"Hmmm ... " he said as if he were actually contemplating this.

"You jerk!" I squealed, as he got up from his chair, scooped me off my feet, and placed me on the couch. He was clearly enjoying this.

"Now, why would I want any other woman when I have the most beautiful woman in the world in my arms?"

Devlin never said generous things to me like that. It was moving. We lay there like that for a long time.

"Brendan, the reason I haven't shared everything with you is because I'm a mother first. I want to tell my children my secret first. It affects them, directly. Then, I'll tell you. I have no reason, not really, not anymore, to not share it with you. Bonnie made me realize that my secrecy could be one of the reasons Alexis has been acting out the way she has. And that's on me. I owe it to my kids to be honest with them. I owe it to you. It's time I started facing up to my past, however painful it may be. Because I'm running out of time ... " I let the words peter out. Even thinking the thought made me sad.

"What do you mean, running out of time?" Brendan asked, turning me around in his arms to face him.

"My mother ... " I started, and then, burst out crying.

"Oh, Imogen, darling, what is it? What about your mother? Have you heard from her? Has something happened?" Brendan was holding me close to him, and I could hear the concern in his voice.

"She's dying."

"What?" Brendan asked.

"She's got cancer. She's not well."

"Wait, I thought you'd had no contact with your parents in twenty years?" he asked, sounding confused.

"I haven't. I found out through a mutual friend. Acquaintance, really. Just before you came into my life. Before this whole mess with the murders happened."

Brendan stared at me and for the first time, I couldn't read his expression or thoughts.

"Then you have to go see her, Imogen. If I've learnt anything from the past few weeks, it's the agony our parents experience when we disappear from them. Nothing, no hurt, no damage, nothing is worth not fixing the situation. And you must do it quickly. While you have time."

I stayed in silence, processing his words.

"I'll come with you," he said. "I'll come with you to Scotland. The moment we put this mess behind us, and we catch the bastard who's doing this to people, we can take the first flight out to your hometown."

"Okay," I said, and then nestled back into his arms. I loved this man. He didn't push for explanations right then and there, which many would have. He just told me what I needed to do. Plain and simple.

"That's why I asked Lexie and Justin to come in for spring break, next weekend. I'm going to tell them everything. It scares the life out of me, how they'll react, but they're old enough now to try and understand. And the moment I tell them, I'll tell you, my darling man," I said, holding him close.

"Okay, Im. I will support you the whole way through," he said. And we fell asleep like that, on the sofa, with the TV blaring the news, trusting in the newfound hope of our relationship and all the affirmations it had offered in such a brief time.

18

SPRING BREAK CAME, and Justin and Alexis were sitting across for me, in my living room, staring expectantly at me.

"So, what's this big secret you've got to tell us, Mum?" Alexis said, facetiously, chewing into an apple.

"Shut up, Lexie. Can't you see Mum's nervous? Let her tell us in her own way," Justin said, irritated at his sister's cavalier attitude, which had now become her calling card when I was around.

"Okay," I said, taking a deep breath, having never experienced such anxiety my whole life. So much was at stake. How could I even begin to say the words?

"Justin, Alexis, the reason I've always been so reticent about my past in Scotland was because ... "

"Yes?" Justin asked, looking intensely curious.

"Okay, first, promise me one thing. Nothing I say leaves this room. You will realize for yourselves, why, when I share what I'm about to," I said, my mind racing.

"For god's sake, Mum? What is it?" Lexie asked, annoyed. "I mean, you'd think you'd murdered someone, the way you're going on."

"That's enough!" I screamed at my daughter. "Do you realize how insensitive you sound? I'm clearly about to share some very important news with you, and all you can bring yourself to do is continue to take potshots at me!" I had tears in my eyes.

"Oh god, Mum, are you alright?" Justin jumped on his feet, and was by my side in an instant, consoling me.

"You're a real jerk, you know that?" he said to his sister. "You've made Mum cry." He was upset.

"It's okay," I said, settling down.

"I left Killin, the village I'm from in Scotland, because my childhood sweetheart had been murdered ... by your grandfather."

There was utter silence in the room.

"What?" Justin whispered.

Even Alexis had gone silent, her face ashen.

"I never went to the police with it. But I knew—had proof— your grandfather was behind the murder of the man I would've spent my life with. Michael, that was his name, Michael and I were to go to university together. The University of Dundee. I was to study medicine, and he, carpentry. We were just about to leave, when he was found drowned in the local river. But I later discovered proof that it was Mark, your grandfather, who was behind Micheal's death. When your grandpa realized I'd found out the truth, he threatened me. He—your grandfather—is not a very nice man. He used to beat my mother, Mary, after one to many drinks at the pub ... "

I let the words trail away into silence. This was the first time I'd recounted what had happened to someone else since I'd left Scotland. It filled me with a sadness that was overwhelming. A floodgate had been opened into my emotions right in front of my children. I had nowhere left to hide. I felt eye contact, overwhelming grief. The tears flowed freely.

"Mum, why didn't you go to the police?" Alexis asked, quietly.

"Because he was my father. Because I was scared. Not for me. I'd made up my mind to leave a long time ago, but I was afraid for my mum. What he'd do to her, if the whole thing came out. He had a way of blaming her for everything. Even his own mistakes. It's hard to explain. A cornered animal is the most dangerous ... "

"Are they both still alive?" Justin asked.

"Yes. But I just found out a few months back that your grandmother is ill, with cancer, and that she's been separated from her husband, your grandpa, for many years now. I need to go home and see her."

"You abandoned her," Alexis said.

"That's enough!" Justin screamed at his sister, whacking her over the head with his hands.

"Stop it. Please, both of you. Yes, Justin. Lexie's right. I did abandon my mother. I was barely eighteen and grieving over the death of the man I was to marry, by the hands of my own father. I escaped. I'm not justifying it, but it's what I could cope with, at the time," I said, my face moist with tears.

"It's okay, Mum. You were young. And that awful man was your father," Justin said, coming over to me and hugging me. That one of my own children would forgive me was like water on a burning bridge, and it comforted my heart.

After a long moment passed, I said, "There's more."

"More?"

"Actually, I really don't even know how to bring this up, because it will sound outlandish, and you'll probably think I'm crazy for sharing it. I only ask one thing of you, before you say anything," I said, turning to my daughter. "Anything hurtful."

"Okay, here goes," I began. I come from a … fellowship. In Scotland. There are many of us there like me, your grandparents belong to it too, and it was the reason Michael ended up dead."

My children were staring at me incredulously. I had nothing to lose. I looked away and continued.

"Have you ever wondered why the NYPD would ask me to work with them, in the capacity of a psychic at that, to help them solve crimes?"

"It was bizarre, Mum," Justin offered, frankly. "But, I don't know what you do with your free time. I thought maybe it was, like, a hobby or something, you'd taken up."

I smiled at my sweet son.

"No, it's not a hobby. It's who I am, at a very fundamental level. And both, you and Lexie have inherited a part of that heritage, as well, as a result."

"Wait, what are you talking about?" he asked.

I finally said the dreaded words out loud, the ones I'd been protecting my children from, for all these years.

"I'm a faerie."

"A what now?" Justin said, balking at me.

"A faerie."

"Mum. You sound insane," Lexie said.

"Let her speak," Justin said, and with such authority, his sister quietened down.

"Remember, last summer, Justin, when you told me you felt like you could read people's thoughts? Have you ever wondered why that is the case?"

He stayed quiet for a long time. "I just thought it was intuition. Strong intuition."

"And Lexie, remember when you told me you knew your classmate Janice was pregnant, even before she'd told anyone. When I'd asked you how you knew, you said something to the effect that you'd forgotten how you'd found out? But I knew. It's because you have a part of the gift. It runs in our veins. The Seelie and Unseelie Faerie Courts ... that's our heritage, I'm half of each, gives us the heightened empathy that we possess. It's obviously much stronger in me, as I am full Faerie, but you both also have half of that heritage. I don't know how it will manifest itself for you. Maybe it will just mean you'll have heightened insight ... or intuition, as you put it, Justin, into situations and people. It's not a bad thing. Well, mostly not."

"What do you mean, mostly?" Justin asked. I could feel my son pulling away from me, and I was frantic not to let that happen. I wasn't prepared to lose both of my children. "The Unseelie heritage comes from your grandfather's side. They're troublemakers by nature. The magic makes them that way," I said, trying not to make eye contact with my daughter.

"Mum ... " Justin began.

"Don't say it," I said. "I know what you both must be thinking. But I'm your mum and you've known me in a way only children can. You're my blood. I don't want you to say anything, but just please think about this for a bit. Look it up on the internet if you must. Of course, that stuff is presented as folklore and the paranormal ... but some of it ... is true."

I didn't know what else to say. I felt like an idiot, but this was my truth. Their truth. And they had a right to know, even if it meant I was pushing away my children from me. My heart was breaking.

And then, Justin said the strangest thing.

244

"Mum. You're the most logical and kind person I know. You've loved me and Lexie unconditionally. You've protected us, taken care of us. I know you. You have no reason to make any of this up. I believe you believe it to be true. Is that enough for the moment? I just need some time to process everything. It's been a lot," he said, looking at me, earnestly.

The flood of relief I felt was overwhelming.

"Oh, of course, darling. This is all I ask," I said, going over to my son and hugging him.

"Thanks for not calling me insane," I said, and laughed, wiping the tear from my face.

"Cool," he said, smiling, and then got up. "I'm gonna hit the books in my room. Call me when dinner's ready, okay?" And that was that with my accommodating son.

My daughter was an entirely different matter.

Before I could say anything, she got up and grabbed her purse, keys, and cell phone, and headed to the door.

"Where are you going?" I asked.

"I'm staying with Dad, Mum, remember? Just heading home," she said nonchalantly as if nothing had happened.

"Don't you want to talk about what I've just said?" I asked, worried.

"The fact that you sound insane, Mum? No, not really," she said.

"Lexie, you *cannot* tell anyone what I've shared, okay? Telling people your grandpa is a murderer could put me in jail, okay? You need to ... "

"Relax, Mum!" she hollered, turning to face me. "I know you think I'm useless. That I'm a spoilt, good-for-nothing daughter who has no morals or scruples, but believe it or not, I know when to keep my mouth shut! You're my mother, for Christ's sake!" she yelled, leaving the apartment and slamming the door behind her.

It was all over. The big reveal. That was it. My kids had heard me out and the world had not exploded around me. Life continued. I felt a sense of relief and lightness I hadn't in a really long time. I could breathe again.

19

THE NEXT EVENING, WITH JUSTIN studying hard and barely leaving his room, I decided to take the Connors up in their surprising offer to have me over for dinner. Brendan would be joining us, but a little late as he'd had an errand to run. I'd offered to come late, after Brendan had returned, but it soon became clear to me that the Connors had wanted to talk to me, alone. I was apprehensive but not nervous, as I made my way up the stairs of the palatial brownstone his parents lived in, on Park Avenue.

I rang the bell and was greeted by a staff member, who ushered me into a decadent living room, filled with paintings and rugs and antiquities from around the world, and a grand piano at the center as well. The place reeked of old money. I sat down gingerly on an elaborately designed sofa but soon stood up when Nancy entered the room.

"Oh, please sit down," she said, staring at me intently, as she made her way to a couch opposite mine. It was a two-seater, and this would give the Connors the vantage of staring at me, quite literally, from the opposite side.

"Thank you for inviting me," I said.

"Well, Frank and I thought it was high time to get to know the mysterious woman our son has been spending so much time with," she offered, without a hint of a smile.

"Not so mysterious, I assure you," I said, smiling, although I really felt like I was on exhibit. Frank Connor soon joined us in the living room and sat next to his wife. Neither smiled. It was discomfiting. In all fairness to them, they'd just had their son returned to them, and already, his attention had been hijacked by a woman in the dubious business of being a psychic, who'd clearly crossed professional boundaries and had latched herself onto a man who was worth millions and millions of dollars. I understood their skepticism, although I knew I had to stand firm and not reveal anything they may find untoward. I was, after all, carrying, not just my secret, but that of their son's.

"Look, Imogen we want to get straight to the matter," Frank said, without even engaging in pleasantries. "You seem nice enough, and I'm to gather you're a mother of two and were married to Devlin, of the real-estate fame and fortune."

"Divorced. We're in the process of getting divorced," I interjected, quickly.

"How awful," Nancy added, pointedly. "He was quite a catch."

I took a deep breath.

"Well, actually, we were both very young when we married, and he hadn't made his fortune yet, so ... "

"What are you saying?" she asked.

"I'm just saying, maybe he found me quite a catch back then, that's all," I offered, only half in jest, hoping to put things in perspective. It turned out to be the wrong move.

"Well, you certainly have impeccable taste in men. Now, you know, with Brendan."

"What are you implying?" I asked.

"Well, you don't seem to have held a regular job in all these years, and just when you're about to get divorced, you latch yourself onto another wealthy man."

"You can understand why my wife might feel a bit suspicious, surely?" Frank interjected.

I didn't expect the evening to be perfect, but I couldn't believe the brazenness of their words. Before I could say anything, Frank continued.

"Where are you from, originally? Is that a hint of a Scottish accent? When we asked Brendan to tell us more about your foreign upbringing, he said he really didn't know much about it."

"I've heard quite enough," I said, standing up. "I'm not a criminal under investigation here. I have more than enough money of my own and am not with your son for any of it. I've fallen in love with him," I felt my cheeks flush with indignation. "As for Devlin, I helped him make his fortune. And we're getting divorced because he was unfaithful to me. As for my Scottish heritage, I would've answered any questions if you'd asked me politely. But I will not be treated in this manner by anyone, I don't care who you are!" With that, I turned to leave, but the expressions on Nancy's face softened, suddenly.

"No! Please don't leave like this. Brendan will be furious with us. We've only just got him back. I'm sorry," she said. I could sense these were words she wasn't in the habit of uttering often.

"We're both sorry," Frank added. "But you've got to understand, us being protective of a son who's just been returned to us." He didn't look at me as he uttered those words.

Despite my anger, I felt sorry for these people. I bottled the anger up inside and grimaced at the thought of spending a long evening ahead with them.

"It's okay," I said, and was just about to sit down, again, when both my cell phone, and that of Frank's, rang almost simultaneously.

It was Max. "Brendan was almost attacked in the park. We've nabbed him, Imogen! I think we've got our man!"

"What?" I said, filled with alarm. "Is Brendan okay?"

"He's fine. We were right there when it happened. The bastard didn't stand a chance," Max said, the excitement spilling over in his voice.

"What's happened to my son?" Nancy screamed out loud.

250

"He's okay, dear," Frank said. "He was attacked, but they were ready. I think they've got him."

At the police station, I ran into Brendan's arms, and he held me tightly.

"Are you okay?" I asked. He nodded.

"What were you doing in the park?" his dad demanded. The three of us had rushed to the station when we'd got the calls.

"Making myself visible, I guess," he offered sheepishly.

"What's the matter with you?" I asked, whacking him over the head, lightly.

"She's right, Brendan? What were you thinking?" Frank seconded my words. "It's one thing to participate in this dangerous and frankly, reckless plan, but entirely another matter to offer yourself up to danger in such an obvious way!" He was really upset.

"How much more do you want to put your mother and I through?" he lamented.

"He was always safe, Mister Connor," Max interjected quickly, trying to diffuse the situation. "But your son does have a mind of his own."

We stayed at the station, all of us, for the next several hours, even as Brendan was tended to by paramedics and as he recounted the tense sequence of events that'd unfolded earlier in the evening.

He'd wanted to visit the pharmacy next to the gym where he worked out, but decided, without warning the undercover cops, to walk directly across the park instead, cutting across Fifth Avenue and entering the park through one of the access routes, even as the sunlight had started waning and the embers of dusk fell like lambent flames upon Central Park. The undercover cops and personal security staff had not been warned of this in the carefully planned itinerary and had been at a loss as to what to do. They couldn't very well go up to Brendan. And so, they followed him, at a discrete distance. Brendan seemed to know his way through the many curving pathways and side routes in the large park, and at times, the cops were alarmed that they might lose him deep within the trees and shrubbery. The crowds had petered out and the further and deeper Brendan went into the foliage, the more isolated they were. But the detectives, luckily, had never lost sight of him. And just when they'd passed the midpoint of the park and were heading into its western regions, out of nowhere emerged a dark and lean figure, heavily cloaked, wearing sunglasses, and with the coat's collars pulled up, right behind Brendan. Brendan heard the slight shuffling of another's feet and felt the hair on his nape stand up, signaling that he was being shadowed. The shuffling grew closer, and just when Brendan, fighting his own animal nature from surfacing, was about to turn around and face the person following him, the cops were on the scene. There were four of them, including his private security detail, and they tackled the cloaked man and had removed his sunglasses, wrestling him to the ground. He'd had a dagger in his coat pocket. But when Brendan made eye contact, he recognized the face instantly. It was him. The killer. The man he'd last seen bludgeoning a woman's head in with a rock. The game was over.

"Did he hurt you?" his mother asked, her voice quivering.

"No, Mom, it was just a scuffle. The police were on him almost immediately, and it was all over in a matter of seconds."

Brendan turned to me and said, "It's him, Im. It's the killer. I recognized his face, instantly."

"We're gonna need you to stick around for a bit, if that's okay? Take a statement from you, and have you positively ID the perp, again, if need be," Alberto interrupted.

"That's fine," Brendan said. "I want to put this behind me and my loved ones, once and for all."

20

THE NEXT FEW DAYS WERE a blur of activity. Brendan had positively identified the killer, but the cinching proof was the dental imprints. They were a perfect match for the attacker's.

Louis Mayfield was a forty-nine-year-old drifter and former mechanic, who'd disappeared soon after his wife's death, fifteen years ago. Foul-play had never been suspected in her death, which had been attributed to suicide, as she'd had a history of mental health problems. She had been found drowned in her bathtub. The neighbors had vouched for Louis, and people soon assumed it was grief over his wife's death that had made him abscond. There was no reason to suspect anyone. But, with further digging, the macabre truth surfaced—his movements coincided with the unsolved murders and disappearances of countless women in the northeast. The NYPD had opened a can of worms, and it looked like Max and Alberto had their hands full with the investigation into the grisly past of someone who was turning out to be, possibly, one of the most notorious serial killers in recent history. Multiple agencies were going to be involved in piecing together the gruesome past of this psychopathic man, and he was finally going to be held accountable by the law. The papers read like something out of a thriller novel. Except this was real. Painfully real. And Brendan's life had almost been destroyed by it.

Brendan had confided in me later that he was so afraid he'd go through his supernatural transition in the park when he'd first sensed the man behind him and was bracing for an attack—that that side of him would be too strong to curtail. But he trusted the cops to do their job and had stilled his nerves and fought his inner nature. And this time, it had worked out. His secret stayed safe. Brendan stayed with his parents for the next few days as he felt it was important to reassure them and calm their frayed nerves. I also wanted to spend some time with Alexis and Justin after the bomb I'd dropped on them. We never spoke of what I'd said that fateful evening a few nights ago, but in the solace, I'd extracted from the companionship of my son Justin, I knew deep within that things would be okay with him. We'd weathered the storm out and now, whatever lay in our future, we could handle together, as a team.

But Lexie proved elusive as ever. She dropped in briefly one evening, and from her monosyllabic responses, I'd gathered it was because she'd forgotten something in the apartment and was there to retrieve it, but she disappeared again, almost immediately, before I could ask her if she was okay. It tugged at my heart all week. Despite the profound breakthrough in the case and the incredible relief, it'd brought me in knowing that the killer was off the streets forever and that Brendan's role in this horrific nightmare had come to an end, feeling distant from my own child made me feel empty like there was a missing piece to my heart, one that only Lexie could make whole again.

The kids were leaving on Saturday, and the week was rapidly drawing to a close. I picked up the phone several times and almost dialed my daughter's number, but stopped myself in the end. I knew that whatever I was seeking from my daughter—it had to come from her. If it took her weeks or months to process all that I'd said, I was willing to wait. I had to wait. It killed me inside, but I had no choice. I had to hunker down and wait it out. But I knew one thing—the look on my daughter's face when I'd pleaded to her to keep what had been said private—it was of fortitude. I knew she wasn't going to tell anyone. I just knew. I felt ashamed that I'd somehow underestimated my daughter all along. Where had we grown apart? Was there something I'd missed along the way, with her?

I was lost in these thoughts when the doorbell rang. There was a smattering of spring showers outside, and the air felt damp and clammy as I opened the door. It was Lexie. She was bawling.

"Oh, my God, what happened?" I asked my daughter, as she ran into the apartment and collapsed on the sofa.

"Darling, what's wrong? Please tell me!" I was panicking. My instincts were to protect her, but I hadn't a clue about what was going on. Lexie wasn't the kind of girl who let her emotions show often. She prided herself on having a thick skin. Something bad had happened.

I sat by her feet on the couch, holding her legs with my hands, and waited patiently for the crying to stop. Justin had come out of his room, on hearing the door slam and the commotion, and also sat on the couch close by and stared blankly at her.

When she'd quieted down, she reached for the tissues and blew her nose. We waited.

"Mum, I've made a terrible mistake," she said.

"What happened?" I asked.

"I thought Samantha was a nice person. She's not! She's just a horrible, gold-digging bitch!" Alexis started crying again.

"Did she say something to upset you?" I asked, concerned.

She shook her head. "Not to me. She's had some of her friends over. And they thought I wasn't in the house. And so, she told them she thought I was a spoiled brat and that she was only tolerating me until she and Dad got married. She actually said, 'Once I marry him and make sure of my place in his life, I'm going to ensure that rotten brat isn't left a single cent.' She also said, 'I've worked too hard to meet a man like Devlin, who can give me anything I want, but his family keeps getting in the way. The stupid wife of his is getting so much already in the settlement, and now, it looks like he'll be supporting his daughter for the rest of his life.' Mum, it was awful. So, when I ran into the room and confronted her, she said, 'This is what you get for eavesdropping on people's private conversations.' Can you believe it, Mum?"

I was frankly not shocked. Samantha had revealed her true nature and motivations, and that was now Devlin's problem, but the way she'd made my daughter feel, that was unacceptable.

"That's not all, Mum. I could've handled that," Lexie said. "But when dad came home from work, and I told him what Samantha had said ... he took her side!"

"What?" I said, shocked.

"He took her side! He told me I needed to grow up soon and get serious about my own life, and that while he didn't mind me staying there, if I were to cross Samantha again, I'd be out on the streets!" The wailing resumed.

My blood boiled. The last few months had revealed Devlin to be a cold and heartless man, a feckless soul, but I had always assumed he drew the line when it came to his children. I was wrong. I couldn't believe his deplorable behavior. I was about to pick up the phone and give him a piece of my mind, when Justin stopped me.

"Mum. Don't. Don't stoop to his level. You're almost free of him; don't give him anything to use against you till the divorce comes through."

Then, he turned to Lexie and said, "Look, I know this is rough. But you do need to grow up, Lexie. You've always had people in your life who've loved you—Mum and me—but you were too caught up with Dad and his whole flighty universe to care. Maybe this will make you really open your eyes and see what you're allowing yourself to become. Take a good look in the mirror. Re-evaluate your priorities. Study hard, be nice to Mum, get a job off-campus, and start to stand on your own feet," said my son.

I couldn't have been prouder of him. I was expecting Lexie to retort with something, but she simply said, "You're right. In any case, I'm never taking another cent from that man again."

"It's not him who's the problem, Lexie," Justin added. "Assholes will be assholes, but it's your choices that define you. Not Dad's."

I wanted to admonish my son for calling his father an asshole ... I wanted to, but I couldn't bring myself to do it. I wanted to say something more, but really, Justin had said it all.

For the first time in years, my daughter allowed me to hug her and hold her in my arms. "Do you want me to go get your stuff from Dad's?" I offered. Frankly, I was scared of what I'd do to him, after treating my daughter that way. His own daughter. But Justin volunteered.

"No, I'll go bring her stuff."

"Will you be okay with him?" I asked, concerned.

"I can handle him," Justin said, dismissing any concerns, and with that, he left the apartment.

"I'm sorry for everything, Mum," Alexis said.

"I know," I said, cradling my little girl in my arms, and finally feeling like she was going to be okay. That we were going to be okay.

21

AFTER SPRING BREAK WAS OVER, and my children had left the apartment, I waited eagerly on Saturday evening for Brendan to visit. So much had transpired, and I couldn't wait to share it with him. I'd missed him and had barely seen him the past few days, and my heart was abuzz with excitement at the possibilities that lay ahead of us. A new dawn. A new beginning. I wasn't used to feeling this way, as a middle-aged woman, and it had me on my feet, readjusting furniture in the apartment, playing music, dancing about, and pouring myself a glass of wine before it was even six. I'd also promised myself that this would be the evening. When I'd come clean to my boyfriend. It was time. Everything was slowly falling into place, and I wanted to keep the momentum going, afraid it would all unravel again.

When the doorbell rang, I opened it and my heart did what it always did on seeing Brendan—it skipped several beats. He was wearing a brown leather jacket, braving the early spring weather by doing away with the winter coat for the evening, and smiled warmly upon seeing me. I ran into his arms like a young girl.

"Whoa! I haven't been gone that long, my darling Im!"

"Oh Brendan!" I gushed. "Everything has been sorted out with my kids. With my daughter, especially. We're good, now!"

"So, you told them your secret?" he asked, getting straight to the heart of the matter.

"Yes, I did," I replied, trying to discern his expression, but he just said, "Finally."

"Yes. It happened. Actually, it went a whole lot better than I thought it would."

"I'm so glad, darling," he said, looking at me but not saying anything.

"And yes, that means it's time I told you too," I stated.

"I'm not pressuring you, please notice!" he exclaimed.

"Oh, I want to tell you. I've been dying to tell you all this while, but call it a mother's instinct. Or her duty. Whatever it was, I had to tell them first. Now, I can share it with you. I need you to sit down," I said, pointing to the couch.

"That bad, is it?" he said, trying to lighten the mood. But I could see he was anxious.

I laughed. "No! It's not bad. Not bad at all, really," I said, sidling up to him on the couch and looking him squarely in the eyes.

"So, the reasons I've shared so little about my life in Scotland, before I came over here, to America, have been two-fold." He nodded solemnly. I knew he'd understand, I just knew. I settled my racing heart and finally started to tell him.

"My father killed my childhood sweetheart. Michael. He murdered him or had someone do it for him." I didn't say anything more.

"Oh, Jesus. Imogen. That's horrid. I don't know what to say. I'm speechless."

"Yes. That's why I ran away to America. Gave up my childhood dreams of becoming a surgeon. I wanted a new start."

"Is he in prison?" Brendan asked. "Your father?"

"No," I said, looking away.

"Why not?"

"Because I never turned him in."

"Oh, Imogen," Brendan said, looking aghast but trying to cover it up.

"I know I made a lot of mistakes back then. The only thing I'll say in my defense is that I was young. And scared. Not for myself, though he did threaten me if I took what I knew to the cops. I was scared for my mum."

When Brendan looked at me in a manner that indicated he didn't understand, I continued.

"Oh Brendan, he was an abusive husband, beating up my mum whenever he got drunk. I was scared, okay? That if I left Killin, and she was stuck with him, and they let him off or worse, the local police didn't believe me, I was scared he'd take it out on her," I admitted, looking at my feet.

"That's why I never went back. I couldn't stand the cowardliness of my own behavior. And didn't know how to face my dear mum. The person I loved the most in the world. For abandoning her with that man. And as time passed, the more difficult it became. More complex. I was an adult, barely, but an adult when it'd happened. I'm pretty sure it's illegal to help cover up a crime, when you know the truth. To not come forward. But, most of all, the strange thing is, Brendan, my mother loved my father. Utterly and completely. Theirs was a special bond."

"How can you say that, Imogen?" Brendan responded agitatedly.

"Okay, so this brings me to the other thing I need to share. My father hated Michael, my boyfriend, because he was not a ... "

"Not a what? And what has that got to do with him abusing your mother? Nothing justifies beating up a woman. Nothing."

"Not a faerie!"

Brendan went silent, staring at me.

"Brendan, I'm a faerie. A supernatural being, myself. That's how I knew of your innocence. My gift is that I can read people. Really, really well, when my instincts are on fire. And they were off the charts when I met you. I knew I'd met another supernatural being when I laid eyes on you. I could read your aura, however you want to put it, and I could see, almost immediately, that you were innocent of those horrific murders."

Brendan stayed silent, staring at me. I looked away.

"My parents come from rival Faerie factions, yin and yang, you could say. I'm half Seelie and half Unseelie Court. They are like denominations, except the kind of Faerie nature is in our blood. My mum is Seelie, my father, Unseelie. The Unseelies ... they're unpredictable. Mischievous. Dangerous, even, in circumstances. But my parents fell in love and married against much opposition from the High Council."

When I noticed Brendan raising his eyebrows, I quickly said, "I'll explain everything. That's why my mum forgave him all those times he beat her. Gave her bruises. She made allowances for his nature, written into his bones and blood, something he couldn't do anything about. And maybe that's why I didn't go to the police. He was my dad, at the end of the day. I told you it's complicated."

I got up and walked to the wine bottle and poured myself another glass. I couldn't bring myself to look at Brendan. To see the disappointment in his eyes.

"I knew it." I heard the words coming from behind and swung around on my heels to face him.

"What?"

"I knew you were special. I now know why," he said, staring at me with sympathetic eyes.

"But Imogen," he said, "I'm sorry to say this, but your dad's an asshole."

"Let's not ... " I started, but he interrupted me.

"I've been fighting my lycanthropic nature my whole life. It's taken me till middle age to realize I could've spared everyone, myself, my parents, years of heartache if I'd just accepted myself as is. I learned to accept my animal nature, my supernatural self because I would've taken the first steps toward controlling it by doing that. Fighting it. And yes, at times, embracing it. Which I have, finally, and with you by my side. "But your father, he'd had love and support and a fellow supernatural being's understanding his whole life. And yet he seems to have taken no steps toward controlling his nature. If that is indeed the place his deplorable behavior stems from. Like is said, some people could just be assholes, plain and simple. Maybe it has nothing to do with his supernatural powers."

I stayed quiet. There was no point arguing. Most of what Brendan was saying was true. Some people were just jerks.

"So, you're a faerie," he said, getting up and moving slowly toward me.

"Yes."

"Does this mean you can cast a spell on me?" he asked, playfully pulling me close to his body.

266

"I think I already have," I said playfully. With that, he kissed me deeply and lifted me in his arms, carrying me into the bedroom

When we made love that night, it was different. It was in the full knowledge that there were no more secrets between us. And that we were kindred spirits, united by our supernatural instincts, and thus, bound together in a way no one else was. We were joyful and unfettered, free of the burden of our secrets, free of unfair branding and labeling, and free to pursue the depths of our love for each other. It was a magical night.

The next morning, I woke up early to the phone ringing. I could feel Brendan stir next to me and answered it quickly, so as not to wake him. It was barely six in the morning.

"Imogen," I said, sleepily, not bothering to check the number.

"Imogen, it's Eoin." His voice shook the remnants of slumber from my mind. I was alert and listening with trepidation.

"I'm afraid I have really bad news," he said.

"What is it?" I asked, feeling a terrible sense of dread at the pit of my stomach.

"It's your mum. Mary. She passed away last night. It was sudden."

I dropped the phone from my hands. I felt the room swim and my heart race. And then a pain one only experiences at the death of a loved one. It overwhelmed me. I didn't have words. I just started screaming. Brendan quickly woke up and tried to wrap me in his arms, as I wept inconsolably. "Mum's dead," I whispered, barely being able to get the words out. And then, I collapsed in his arms. Brendan rocked me gently, back and forth, as the minutes ticked by, and I could hear the faint whisper of Eoin's voice on the phone, frantically and repeatedly, calling out my name.

ENJOYED THIS BOOK?

I WOULD LOVE TO HEAR FROM YOU.

Thank you so much for reading my book. I hope you enjoyed reading it as much as I did writing it!

Book reviews are a precious tool for getting the attention of new readers. Unfortunately, as an independent author, I have a limited budget for promotion, and, most probably, you will never see my book cover on the subway or on TV.

But I do have something much more powerful and effective than an unlimited budget to spend, and it's something publishing firms would kill to get their hands on: my readers!

I experienced firsthand that honest reviews help attract other people like you, which is why you are reading this. If you enjoyed this book, could you help me writing even better ones in the future?

I will be eternally grateful if you could dedicate a minute to leave a review using the link below:

http://readerlinks.com/l/1901657

JOIN MY MAILING LIST

Let's keep in touch! Be the first to receive cover reveals, sneak peaks, promos and much more.

Subscribe here: https://www.subscribepage.com/miaconnor

I hate spam myself and your email is safe with me. It will not be transferred to third parties or used for other purposes than talking about our beloved books. Also, you can unsubscribe at any time.

STAY UPDATED

Join Mia Connor's Facebook group

READ THE PREQUEL

https://BookHip.com/WSAAAQC

OTHER TITLES IN THE SAME SERIES:

Midlife Dramatic

Midlife Hypnotic

Midlife Ecstatic

Midlife Cathartic

Midlife Magnetic

Made in the USA
Coppell, TX
13 October 2021